Digging

up the

Dead

A Viv Fraser Mystery

V. Clifford

FOR RHCC

Other Viv Fraser Novels

Beyond Cutting

Finding Tess

Non Fiction

Freud's Converts

Chapter One

Was he scolding her? Viv Fraser hunched in the doorway of the village paper-shop, and watched in frustration as her friend Geraldine stood on the pavement opposite, with torrential rain bouncing all around her. There was no indication, from the couple's body language, of love, unconditional or otherwise. The man with his hands thrust deep inside his jacket pockets and his large square jaw jutting out from an oversized hood. He towered above Geraldine and from where Viv was standing he seemed intent on violating that invisible boundary which no one should transgress. Geraldine displayed none of the confidence that Viv was accustomed to: she looked strained, her knuckles white as she gripped the strap of her leather shoulder bag. Geraldine's eyes roved over the pavement seeking anything to keep her attention away from him. Suddenly he stepped closer, wrapped an arm around Ger's shoulders and guided her back towards her car. At first Viv thought Ger was objecting, but she conceded and allowed herself to be led. He glanced back towards Viv but his hood prevented her from getting a proper look at him.

Viv, unconvinced that Ger was doing the right thing, decided that he was bad news, but was in no position to interfere. As soon as they were out of sight she pulled up her own hood and raced back towards the cottage. Doune was an unplanned village with a hotchpotch of architectural styles. Small elegant Georgian houses stood cheek by jowl with bothies, once lived in by pistol makers or bakers with extended families. The Catholic Church, positioned high off the road with a wall marking its boundary, was where Viv turned off the main street into the kind of lane that you'd find decorating a shortbread tin. She passed a row of cottages on her left, and continued over one of General Wade's hump-backed bridges, moving like a fell runner, avoiding potholes rapidly filling with muddy water flowing from the field above. Soon she was through the estate gates, up a long drive, part of an old military road, with leafy branches overhanging one side, and where deep tyre ruts desperately needed a top up of gravel to bring them level with the grassy mound in the middle, a mound that made it impossible for any car other than a 4x4 to reach the top without damaging its undercarriage.

Dripping wet, she reached the stone cottage and huddled beneath the porch at the side door. The sound of Molly, Sal's bearded collie, barking broke into her concerns for Ger. She toed off her boots and shook her jacket before taking them inside. The tack-room, once home to halters, yokes, and saddles, was now a drying room for Sal's outdoor gear. Walls panelled with dark varnished tongue and groove were studded with large brass hooks laden with ropes, chalk bags, and an assortment of garish waterproof clothes. What could be seen of a flagstone floor had evidence of hobnails on a few of its slabs, but was otherwise crowded with neat rows of boots and trainers; lots of stuff but everything in its place.

She relished the warmth of under-floor heating rising through her socks. Molly bounced and twirled round her as if she'd been away for hours. She cuddled Moll and rubbed her ears as they rolled onto the sofa in mutual admiration, until her phone vibrated perilously close to the edge of the table, and she abandoned play to grab it before it fell to the floor. She missed the call, but recognized Jules' number, who, had she been desperate to speak to Viv, wouldn't have given up so quickly.

She padded through to the kitchen, flicked the switch on the kettle, still nervous of using the Aga. She chewed on her lip and hugged her upper arms, relieved that the rain beating on the conservatory roof couldn't get to her. It had taken a few days to settle here, but now she'd relaxed, as much as she ever could, into the slow rhythm of her days. Meeting Ger was a fly in the ointment that she hoped to shake off. What was not to like about being with a dog whose enthusiasm couldn't be matched? And catching up on reading that she'd been too tired to concentrate on was no bad thing either.

Viv almost missed a second call but reached it as her message service kicked in. It was Mac's number. She called straight back. 'Hey, Mac! How you doing? You're not supposed to . . .' Mac's Sunday name was DCI Marcus Marconi. He headed up the NTF (National Task Force), originally set up as a counter-terrorism branch of Police Scotland with reaches into National Security. Viv

7

had been 'invited' not to ask about details. She'd done the odd job for them and satisfied with her results they'd asked her back again and again.

Mac's voice sounded tinny, on a speaker-phone in his car. 'I'm in the area and wondered if you'd like a late lunch?'

'I've had lunch, but swing by. I'll stick the kettle back on.'

'Great. Ten minutes.' He hesitated. 'Is Sal back yet?'

'No. Her flight's delayed in Houston so she's not getting in until tomorrow. Mightily pissed off I might add, but there's nothing she can do. Did you want to see her?'

'I'll explain when I get there.'

Intrigued, she briefly mused on Sal's relationship with Mac, until she noticed that she was tidying on his behalf, folding newspapers, plumping cushions and gathering mugs that had built up over the week. She reminded herself that she wasn't expecting her auntie Jeannie, her mother's sister, whose ability to seek and find dust was unparalleled. She shook her head to relieve her mind of faces from the past, intruders who appeared when she least expected them.

Viv told Molly that they were having a visitor but unsurprisingly the dog made no attempt to move from her snuggled position on the sofa. Her ears twitched when Mac's car pulled up, and as Viv walked toward the front door she deigned to bang her tail. Hearing Mac's voice was a test too far, and she bolted to greet him as he came in the front door.

'Hey, Moll.' Mac bent down and fussed with the dog until she was satisfied and trotted back into the sitting room. 'She's looking great.' Then turning to Viv with raised eyebrows. 'Not looking too shabby yourself. Enjoying the rest?'

Viv grinned. 'What are you after, you charmer?' She gestured for him to follow her into the kitchen, where a pot of coffee stood covered with a tea cosy.

'I've got the weekend off. Thought I'd come and do a bit of work on my place. It's badly in need of some TLC. But if this rain continues it will put paid to me doing the outside stuff I'd planned.'

She handed him a mug and smiled. 'I didn't have you down as a DIY man.'

'I'll bet there's a lot you don't have me down as.' He smirked and nodded to the conservatory. 'In here?'

'Sure, grab a seat.'

The windows were running with condensation, making it impossible to enjoy an uninterrupted view of parkland and mature specimen trees that lay beyond. Viv went in search of a cloth to clear them. Once she'd returned the cloth to the kitchen, she said, 'So what's on your mind?'

Mac blew over the top of his coffee before taking his first sip. 'It's probably nothing.'

She hated it when he did this. 'You wouldn't be here if it was nothing. Stop bullshitting.'

He raised a conciliatory hand. 'Okay. Well, we got a call about an archaeological site this week. Up on Sheriffmuir.' He waved in the direction behind his head. 'Central have a brilliant team up here, but there were so many bits of bodies turning up that it became clear that we were dealing with . . . I'm too nervous to say this out loud, 'cause if the media got hold of "mass grave" they'd whip themselves into a frenzy.'

Viv raised her eyebrows. 'So, multiple bodies? Old or new?'

'That hasn't been established yet. And anyway how old is old? We wouldn't normally get to know much about this kind of thing, but when the body count rises, and journos get interested, we're forced to take a look. And I have to confess that since I know the area I was more than a little intrigued. Don't suppose you fancy a bit of a hike?'

'Where exactly is this site?'

'It's a huge area. I've got map references, but I'd rather just drive up and see the lie of the land for myself. It's near, maybe even on, the battle ground at Sheriffmuir. Not that anyone seems to know where the actual battle took place.'

Viv stared out at the rain, assessing the sky. 'In that?' She pointed outside.

'Fair-weather investigator or what?'

'You accusing me of being soft? I'm no fair-weather freak, but let me check the forecast. I've already been soaked today.'

Viv nipped upstairs to where she'd left her laptop. On returning she said, 'Wifi's not great here and in this weather it'll be even worse.' She moved the laptop from place to place until she found a hot spot where the signal kicked in. 'Look, it says it's going to clear later in the afternoon, why don't we leave it until then?'

Mac shrugged. 'Fair enough. The bones won't be going anywhere. I'll go to mine, switch the heating on and disturb the mice. The place is bound to be damp. I haven't been up for weeks.'

Viv, distracted by the novelty of having an internet connection only heard the word "mice". 'Did you say mice? Shit! I'd forgotten that small country matter of indoor rodents.' She screwed her face up and shook her head to rid her mind of its mousey vision. 'Nothing's coming up about your bodies, which means they can't be that interesting, or there's tons of other grisly news. Anyway you go and do your stuff, and I'll catch up on my emails before I sort out the wood situation here.' She gestured towards the stove. 'Sal's none too hardy and I'd like the place to be cosy when she gets home.'

'Very domestic.'

Viv placed her hands on her hips, and smiled. 'We can but try. The chance of me salvaging any dry wood and hauling it in here is remote. What's with these April showers dipping into May?' She ruffled her hair. 'What time, then?'

Mac blew out a breath. 'It's two thirty now. Say half four, five? We could grab something to eat at the Sheriffmuir Inn after if you like?'

'Sounds like a plan. Do we need to book? Friday night could be busy.'

He pointed at her laptop screen, 'Since you're already up and running could you Google the number and give them a ring?'

'Sure.'

Viv watched as Mac scanned the room. Bookshelves occupied all available floor space. Old paintings and prints crammed every patch of wall that wasn't glass. 'You've got this place looking . . . lived in. As if it's a permanent home and not just a weekend place.'

Viv and Sal had been taking tentative steps to becoming an item, but it was early days and she could see his statement for the fishing expedition that it was. She shook her head. 'As you well know, none of this is my doing. Sal's aunt left it more or less as you see it. Sal's done very little to change the character, although tons of insulation and the under-floor heating in the boot-room is a godsend.' She shrugged. 'It is really comfortable, and the views when you can see them, are spect . . .' Then she remembered that Mac and Sal went way back. 'Sorry, granny and sucking eggs.'

He grinned, drained his coffee, and wandered through to the kitchen. 'Dishwasher yet?'

'You're looking at her. Just leave it on the top.'

But he rinsed it under the tap and set it on the draining board.

'Very domestic!'

'I'll pick you up at half four, five.' He dried his hands with a towel on the rail of the Aga. 'Nice heat.'

Viv nodded and guided him towards the door. 'See you later then.'

Chapter Two

She spent the next hour sorting through emails, responding where necessary, before hauling as much wood as she could manage into a log sack. Despite straining her trapezius in the process, she stacked the logs neatly along the wall of the conservatory. She knew she should have washed the blankets from the dog's bed, but relished the reassuring smell of wet dog lingering in the room, besides 'should' was super-ego shit, so instead she scrolled the internet again for archaeological digs in the Central Belt. The only piece that she could find was by the local newspaper, and referred to a council application, which had been rejected then appealed, and finally got permission to go ahead. The first spade had only gone in on the Tuesday of that week.

The archaeologists, from Sheffield University, had a specific interest in spurs. Viv smiled, thinking of the football club, but doubting academics would even have heard of them. How many of the soldiers in the eighteenth century had been on horseback? Surely most of them were on foot? Returning to the article, Sheffield Uni had requested to do a survey of Sheriffmuir battle site with metal detectors and some local official had deemed such equipment 'inappropriate' and 'unprofessional'. Viv chuckled, knowing that someone had had to swallow a gut load of pride and allow the work to go ahead.

13

Was that a good enough reason for a local to want to throw a proverbial spanner in the archaeologists' work? She thought not, but made a note of the people from the article, just in case. After checking out their names on Google and finding nothing of interest, she realized she'd wasted enough time and decided to give Moll a quick walk before Mac picked her up. She yanked on wellies and a dry jacket, and strode off towards the Quarry Park, the dog not far from her heels.

As forecast, the rain had stopped and the sun sneaked out intermittently from behind clouds that, although higher and lighter, didn't engender complete confidence. She crossed the stile, and pulled up a special door built for Moll. The dog had once jumped the fence and caught her belly on a strip of barbed wire. All barbed wire had since been removed, but Sal wasn't one for taking chances, and the doggy door was added, eliminating all possibility of another accident.

Viv skirted the perimeter of the field in front of the cottage. The imposing edifice of Doune Castle sat high and proud on her right. The Ardoch Burn roared and tumbled over boulders at the base of the castle rock. Cries from a pair of buzzards were drowned out by a cawing rookery that they'd disturbed. The ground, still poached by last season's cattle, made walking hard going. Sal had mentioned that the livestock wouldn't arrive until the end of the month, so Viv was free to wander without fear of disturbing pregnant cows, or worse, cows protecting young calves. Lush grass stood well above her ankles, and with each step the smell of late spring tickled her nostrils and began to irritate her.

A townie to the core, she drew in a breath, making an effort to enjoy it. She told herself how impressive it was to have such rich pasture on the doorstep, but immediately countered this with the fact that she was becoming overwhelmed by such bounty. The dog trotted ahead, never quite pulling out the full reach of the extending lead, and snuffled along the edge of a stock fence, which, to Viv's relief, prevented Moll from getting to the burn.

Viv jumped onto a huge square concrete plinth, a solid reminder of the army's presence during and after the Second World War. The estate, requisitioned by the MOD and used as a prisoner of war camp, had lots of concrete bases where Nissen huts had been erected and could still be found if you cared to scrape back the nettles. From the plinth it was an easy leap over the fence and into the next field, known as the River Park, for obvious reasons since the Ardoch and the Teith, a wide, menacingly choppy salmon river, acted as its boundaries. Not desperate to go far, since Mac had hiking in mind, she continued to the beach, an area that wasn't so much a beach as a breach in the old bank wall which had silted up, creating a sheltered area. On previous days she'd sat there out of the wind and watched the odd fish display. Not today, though. She about turned and headed across the paddock, the most direct route back to the cottage.

Half way back she stopped, her eyes transfixed on a heron as it struggled to take to the sky, its harrowing call as close as you'd get to a pterodactyl. Buzzards, heron, salmon, and even Moll – she'd seen more animals in her few days here than she'd see in as many months in town.

By the time she opened the door to the cottage, discomfort of all things country oozed from her pores. She blew out her breath trying to rid herself of the desire to escape, to return to town, her natural comfort zone where carbon monoxide in palatable doses, high buildings and the endless footfall of people on pavements pock-marked by gum, satisfied her craving for anonymity. She hadn't heard a single siren since she'd arrived. The quiet was too disconcerting for words.

She dried off Moll's paws, gathered essentials into a rucksack, then nipped to the loo. She'd just finished ruffling her hair and rubbing Vaseline onto her lips when she heard Mac's car on the gravel outside. 'Shit!', definitely too late now to pin a note to the porch and take off. With the clunk of his car door, she knocked on the bedroom window and gestured for him to come in. They met at the bottom of the stairs.

She heaved a frustrated sigh.

He raised his eyebrows. 'You okay?'

'Yeah, yeah.' Resigned. 'I'm nearly there. Just have to leave Moll some food then we're off.

Chapter Three

Mac's Audi 4x4 looked and smelled as if it had just left the showroom.

Viv, conscious that she had grubby boots on for the walk said, 'You okay with me getting in with these?' She held up her foot.

'Sure. Someone has to christen it.'

Viv rearranged a stiff, foot-well shaped cardboard sheet designed to protect the carpet from the mucky soles of an unsuspecting test driver. She stamped her feet to clean the thick treads before jumping in, but she'd only loosened old dirt. Hundreds of little cakes of mud escaped from her soles and tipped off the edges of the cardboard onto immaculate black carpet. She winced. 'Oh God. Sorry about that.'

Mac grinned. 'Honestly, don't fret. It'll give me something to do this weekend.'

'It is the weekend. I thought you were going to work on your cottage.' Viv had never been to Mac's country retreat and knew nothing about it other than what he'd said earlier. 'I'll give you a hand if you like. Sal has a super vacuum that'll sort that in a jiff.'

He nodded, 'I said, don't fret. It'll be a whole lot worse by the time we've trampled over Sheriffmuir.'

They drove the three miles from Doune, through Dunblane, Viv fighting a sense of imprisonment. The countryside glistened as rays of sunlight broke through high, scudding cloud. They turned onto a steep winding road, sign-posted to Sheriffmuir. High walls or tight evergreen hedges camouflaged grand residences, originally the country retreats of Stirling and Glasgow merchants, upgraded now, with electric gates to keep out the proletariat. Further on, these posh suburbs gave way to open fields and eventually to rough moorland. Mac pulled over at a field gate with couch grass growing over its base. It hadn't been opened any time recently. Viv raised her eyebrows in a question.

Mac grinned, 'We won't be long.'

A large stone monument stood at the edge of a conifer wood a short distance ahead. Mac locked the car and while he sorted out the zip of his jacket, Viv wandered over to read the detail on the plaque at the monument's base. Erected to commemorate those lost in the battle, it had dates and names embossed on metal. She knew the history of the battle was unclear, that it hadn't been as simple as Scots against English, or Government troops against Jacobites. The Scots were a fickle lot and she'd read that lots of families, as with other famous Scottish conflicts, had sons on both sides.

They walked north over rough ground, some of it boggy with thick tussocks, which forced them to take high steps. Land that looked flat enough from the safety of the car was a completely different story when walking it. Deep undulations meant that there wasn't a clear view, but Mac seemed to know where he was going, and eventually the dig came into sight. A group of people stood beneath a large but flimsy white tent that was flapping in the breeze. Most of them were dressed in Goretex, a wise precaution for spending hours on a Scottish moor.

Mac knew the DI from Central and it took a few minutes of banter before he introduced Viv as a friend and forensic specialist. She smiled at this suitably vague label. Increasingly Viv was employed as a cyber analyst, but having a PhD on Freud and psychoanalysis had certainly made her a useful unofficial profiler for Mac and his specialist team, not to mention a sounding board for Sal who was official.

They were both handed a sealed bag containing overalls, a sign that they'd accepted Viv as one of them. She and Mac skirted round the edge of the nearest trench until a female introduced herself as an osteoarchaeologist and pointed to a few ochre sticks poking out from the peat. Mac lay on the ground and stretched over to get a better look. The heavy rain earlier had left the bones standing proud in the mud.

'Mac, I may be stating the obvious . . .' Viv shrugged. 'But I suppose someone has to. That bone.' She pointed to the one furthest away. 'Is it much paler than the others, or is it just me?'

'D'you think?' He moved towards the item she was pointing at. 'Yeah, from this angle you could be right. What are you thinking? Newer body?'

'Too early to speculate, it just caught my eye. The others seem much darker and thinner.'

Viv stepped round to the other side of the trench and said, 'Yeah, it's definitely different from the other bones. Maybe it hasn't been in the ground as long as the others? Or maybe it's a different kind of bone?'

At this another archaeologist stepped forward. 'We've already ascertained that some of the bones are newer than others. The point is how new. And whether we're talking archaeology or forensic.'

Mac turned his head up, 'Well, that's why we're here. Let's take a look at what you've already got out of the ground.'

The DI interrupted. 'Too late. It's gone off for testing.' He sidled up close enough to Viv for her to smell alcohol on his breath. He continued. 'We were eager to get results and the lab was about to close for the holiday weekend.' He smirked. 'Not any more they're not. Said they'll do what they can asap.'

'How much has been recovered of that paler bone?' Mac pointed into the mud. The DI shrugged, turned to the archaeologist and nodded.

'There's quite a bit of all the different shades. Peat is usually quite kind to bodies and leaves them relatively intact, but these poor souls look as if they were left exposed to the elements, not actually buried.' He shrugged. 'At first I wondered if they'd been ploughed up, but if they had they'd have been spread over a wider area. Then I thought that perhaps they'd been collected and dumped. As you see, nothing is that far beneath the surface.'

'That's why we called you guys immediately. At first we thought it could be a midden, but sadly not. So far they're all human. There are a few animal bones but they are further over and probably recent, a dead sheep perhaps?' He pointed beyond the tent.

Mac said, 'So the bones were brought here from elsewhere and unceremoniously dumped?' He furrowed his brow. 'Weird.'

The archaeologist shrugged, 'Too early to say. If they are old enough, we'll have to remove every one of them and reassemble what we can before we'll know how they died. Then maybe we can work out the where. But at this depth, they're certainly not ancient and there's no evidence of anything ceremonial.'

'I thought bodies were preserved in peat?' Mac scratched his head.

'They are. The skin, hair, internal organs are all . . . pickled so to speak. But bones are often the first to perish. I mean they still take a while to decompose, but those,' he pointed at the little bits sticking through the mud, 'can't have been there all that long in archaeological terms.'

'Ah, but how long is "that long"? Are we talking decades, or even hundreds of years?'

'I'd guess they've been in there for decades at least.'

Then Mac turned to the DI. 'So we've still no idea whether this is an incident for you guys or . . .?' He left his question hanging.

While Mac was engaged with the DI, Viv wandered round to the next trench, which hadn't been so well covered and now contained a deep dark muddy pool. At the water's edge she noticed a tiny fleck of what appeared like dark red plastic sticking out of the wall of the trench. She knelt down and with gloved hands prodded at the mud around it.

To her dismay the object slipped out and into the water. 'Shit!'

The guy that seemed to be the senior archaeologist shouted, 'What's she doing? This is still our dig.'

Viv stood up. 'Sorry, I just saw a . . .'

He shouted to one of the others. 'Get her out of there and find what she's dislodged.'

A young woman in charcoal grey waterproofs and oversized heavy boots made an ignore-him-face and trudged straight into the trench following the direction that Viv was pointing. She rooted around in the puddle with a sieve and after three dips she retrieved the small object that had fallen into the water. Viv, relieved, blew out a breath that she'd been unaware of holding. The woman climbed back out and poked at the article.

No idea what she was looking at, Viv shook her head, but felt compelled to ask. 'Any idea what it could be?'

The woman smiled. 'I'm guessing we've got a button, still attached to a piece of something, could be leather or . . . Here, hold this and I'll mark the exact spot on the ground and on the map.' Viv held the sieve containing the muddy, rusty thing and felt a wave of satisfaction. Freud believed that psychoanalysis was the archaeology of the mind, and she felt as pleased now as she had at her first psychological revelation. She tried to get Mac's attention but he was occupied with his colleague.

The woman returned and put in a stake with a small yellow flag where Viv had prodded. 'Lucky you.' She smiled. 'I've been on my knees in that trench for five days now and found two old

McEwan's Export tins. You come along and barely glance into it and find . . .' She stopped and poked at the item in the sieve again. 'Could be the button off a garment.' She grinned. 'Better not speculate.'

Viv raised her eyebrows in surprise. 'Oh, my God. You must hate me.'

'Nah, you're all right. We'd have found it once we'd drained this anyway. But I'll get it cleaned up and see if we can get an idea of how long it has been in the ground. No point in guessing.' She wiped her nose on the back of her hand and smiled at Viv. 'It's exciting whoever finds it.'

Viv nodded, grateful for the woman's generosity. 'Suppose so.'

She and the woman with her sieve sauntered over to the tent where a trestle table was set up with basins of water, and a selection of tooth and nail brushes. Viv watched as she began loosening cakes of mud from the object, first dipping it into the water and then rubbing it gently with her finger; a painstaking operation. Viv looked round and saw that Mac was crouched by the bones again.

As she approached him he jumped back to his feet and brushed off his gloved hands. 'You know anything about peat bog bodies?'

She shrugged. 'A little. I read a bit about Tollund Man, and a couple of others found recently in Ireland. But these aren't bog bodies.' She pointed to the bones. 'Bog bodies were usually sacrificial. They wouldn't have been all lumped together like that. That's more like a mass grave. We are on a battlefield after all.'

'Yes, but Dr . . . you're never going to believe this, Crippen, over there, said that he doesn't think they've been here for millennia; centuries perhaps, maybe even decades, but they're not ancient. Until the dates are clear, recent foul play is still an option.' Mac's phone rang, and he wandered away with his finger in one ear as he answered it.

He closed the call and said, 'So much for a holiday weekend. I've got to take a look at another site. Coming with me?'

'Yeah, but what about . . .'

Mac was already stripping off his overalls and heading back in the direction of his car.

Viv shouted after his retreating back. 'You pretending I have a choice? I'd have a serious walk to find transport back to Doune.'

He grinned and threw over his shoulder, 'Don't worry, I can drop you off. But I think you'll be interested in coming with me. There's another grave find. This time on the Lake of Menteith.'

Viv's eyes brightened and she grinned, tripping as she stepped out of her own overalls, then trotting to catch up with him.

'So what's going on there?' He gestured towards the tent.

Viv looked back over her shoulder at the woman with the button, and shrugged and changed the subject.

'So, more bones. Can't be a coincidence, can it? Two archaeological digs get the go ahead in the same week, and both expose piles of bone. Me? I don't think so.'

Chapter Four

Viv's interest was definitely piqued and she continued skipping to keep up with him. 'Was it just me or did you think that some of that bone looked brand new?'

Mac nodded. 'I thought so, but Crippen . . .' He shook his head. 'You'd think he'd change that by deed poll. Anyway, he said that bone's colour is influenced by many things, including the age of the skeleton when it went into the ground, as well as the length of time it has been in the ground. If it belonged to a teenager it's likely to be less porous than an older one. The more porous the more . . .'

'Yeah, yeah, I get it.'

Mac had slowed as if he had another question. He looked back towards the dig then across the boggy landscape to a small stone-built house with a few out-buildings sitting on its own, no trees for shelter, its position bleak and unforgiving. It looked as if it had been there for a long time, in some shape or form. Mac pulled out his Harvey map. Viv was impressed. Sal had a few at the cottage and they were almost indestructible. The wind was getting up and whipped the map. Viv grabbed a corner, so that between them they could find exactly where they were.

Mac pointed to a name, 'Bog House'.

There were ruins marked next to it, so Viv had guessed

correctly. There had been something on the site for a long time. A spring or a well was also marked adjacent to the rubble.

'Worth a look. You thinking what I'm thinking?' He looked at his watch.

Viv nodded. 'Not far to carry the odd dead body.'

'That's my girl!' He dodged the punch that Viv threw at his arm.

'Patronising sod!'

He dodged another attempt to swing at him. 'Just sayin'.'

Sniggering, he took off across the moor and she jogged after him towards the collection of shabby buildings. It was hard going clearing tussocks of reeds and couch grass but they were fit, and since running was their default setting they relished the challenge. After five minutes they'd made it to the yard with good colour rising in their cheeks. Viv noted a pathetic wisp of smoke coming from the cottage chimney. The rear of a pick-up truck stuck out from a small wooden shack with a rusty tin roof at the far end of the yard, a hopeful indication that someone was at home. Viv wondered if the cottage had once had a thatch. She noticed that the quoins on the front entrance changed colour and size half way up, and the remains of an old lintel remained in the stone work three quarters of the way up, a sign that the entrance had once been lower.

Viv smiled and chewed on her lip. People often thought that the Scots were a miniature race, but the purpose of the low door or entrances was defence. You couldn't draw a sword effectively and duck at the same time. A house or rather, bothy, as this had probably always been, exposed out here on the moor, would've been susceptible to attack. If it was standing in 1715 when the battle was fought, the countryside would have been teeming with people, walking, or on horseback, some with carts full of their wares, looking for shelter or sustenance.

Mac broke into her reverie. 'What are you thinking, Viv?'

'Just that all this,' she spun round, holding her arms out like a dervish, three hundred and sixty degrees, until a gust of wind caught her hair and wrapped it round her chin and face, 'All this space would once have had loads of folk coming and going. Not the odd one or two having pub food at the inn back there.' She waved carelessly at the Sheriffmuir pub. 'The community in Dunblane was thriving then, which meant money, goods, and people, lots of them. Traders moving north and south would have passed this way.' She tried to push her hair back but again the wind got the better of her. 'Hard to believe it seeing this desolate place now. Sheep fodder. That's all it's worth now.' Viv saw the curtain on the right of the front door twitch and nodded to Mac. 'They're expecting us.'

Mac turned and stared at the cottage. 'D'you think they'll be expecting archaeologists?'

'We sort of are. Digging for answers to crimes. Got to be archaeology of some kind.'

He grinned. 'Nice. I like it.'

They trudged across the muddy yard and Mac knocked on the

door. Nothing. He knocked again. Nothing. Then the engine of the pick-up gunned and they stepped round to the side and watched as a red-haired woman reversed it out into the yard.

Mac put his hand up to stop her from driving straight past them. She reluctantly drew to a halt but kept the engine idling, and grudgingly rolled down the window.

'Hi there. Just wondered if you had any interest in the dig over yonder?'

Viv, surprised by Mac's accent and the word 'yonder', looked away. Was he trying for yokel or what? The woman could be a professor for all he knew.

But when she spoke Viv realized he'd got the tone just right, professor or not.

The woman responded. 'Nah. Too busy for watching what others are up to.'

'D'you mind me asking what you do up here?'

The woman's hair, showing white flecks at the temples, was tied back but wayward strands wisped across her forehead. Her face was weather-beaten and her hands hadn't seen a manicure in a while but these were not enough to distract from stunning, piercing blue eyes. Viv could see that she'd once been incredibly beautiful. She had good teeth, but a smile without mirth exposed a little dent on the right hand side of her bottom incisor. Viv recognized the wear; her dad had been a pipe smoker. She glanced into the truck and spotted a Meerschaum, the Rolls Royce of the pipe world, in the well at the front.

The woman stared at Viv as she answered Mac's question with a shake of her head. 'Look around. What does it look like?' Then in a weird voice she muttered, 'Sherpa.' And a black and white collie jumped from the back of the truck into the front seat. 'She give you a clue?'

'Shepherd?'

'Good guess.'

'You'll have been out all hours then with the lambing?'

Viv was impressed. She'd noticed the lambs up on the hill but wouldn't have thought he'd put two and two together so quickly.

The woman screwed up her eyes but didn't speak.

Mac was not for leaving empty handed and continued. 'You lived here long?'

'All my life.'

'So it's a family home?'

She screwed up her face again and glared at him as if he was stupid, then turning to Viv, she fixed piercing irises on her and in a proud tone said, 'Course. Six generations. Not all shepherds, mind.' And for the first time the notion of fun danced across her face. Before Mac could ask any more questions she stepped on the accelerator and shot out of the yard, forcing them to jump back. They stared at the rear of the truck, then at each other in shock.

'Guilty conscience?' Mac scratched his face.

'Or just anti-social? I might have done the same myself . . . were I not so nosey. She didn't want to find out who, why or what we were here for.'

'Don't give her too much credit for simple uninterest. Remember, she did try to take off. There's always a why in there.'

'You think there's anyone else inside?'

'Try the door again if you like?'

She did, but nothing doing.

The road that the woman took ran the full length of the boundary of her property, and for half a mile she would be able to keep an eye on them as she drove towards the Dunblane road.

Viv tried the door again but still no one answered. They had a quick peek around the outside but only saw what you'd expect to see in any small-holding – a couple of hens scratching at very little, bales of hay, plastic buckets probably used for sheep feed. An old fridge stood at the back of the shed. Viv checked inside. It contained vaccines and a glass bottle with clear liquid in it which she stuck under her nose. She didn't smell anything.

Viv strolled back to where Mac was crouching on the ground. 'There's more than one vehicle usually parked here.'

'They're bound to have a quad-bike for checking their stock. It's not like the old days when the shepherd took up a crook and walked the hills in search of lost lambs.' She nudged Mac's arm. 'C'mon, let's take a quick look to see if we can find the well. I saw it marked on the map; think it's over this way.' She wandered off into the field at the back of the house. Mac followed, but after a few minutes of searching they found nothing that could constitute a well or spring, although it was difficult to tell because the ground underfoot was saturated. Perhaps that was the only thing that was left of it, an even wetter area in what was already bog.

Chapter Five

'Time to head to the Port of Menteith, and see if we can hitch a lift across to the island. Historic Scotland's ferry'll have finished by now, but hopefully one of the fisheries guys will be intrigued enough with the comings and goings today to take us.'

Viv nodded. 'It's bound to be the most interesting thing that's happened in the area for . . . how long?'

'Watch it, townie. City folks always assume that nothing happens in the country, and you know what – they'd be wrong.'

'Since when did you become one of the county set?'

Mac snorted, 'You haven't seen my country pad yet, have you?'

'Nope. But if the batch pad in town is anything to go by . . .'

He didn't rise, just shook his head as they made their way back to the car via the track, which was easier going than the moorland. As they neared the road, a delivery van turned in and stopped. The chirpy driver said, 'Maggie not in, then?'

Mac and Viv exchanged a glance and Mac answered. 'Not that we know of. But if she's the woman with the pick-up, she headed towards Dunblane a few minutes ago.'

'No worries, I've got a parcel for her.' The driver lifted a package from the passenger seat of his van and held it up. He read the huge black writing, 'For Maggie O' The Bog.' Then, laughing, 'That's what folks round here call her, but I didn't realize she was known further afield as that.' He laughed again, exposing dark pink gums with small yellowing teeth, 'Maggie O' The Bog, eh!' before continuing on his way down the track, grinning and shaking his head.

Mac shrugged. 'Great name. If you're going to have a nickname you might as well have one that leaves its mark.' He repeated the name. 'Maggie O' The Bog.' As he said it a questioning look crossed his face. 'There's something familiar about it . . . Nope, no idea what, though. Never mind, let's get a move on.'

Mac knew his way around the roads, which made Viv think his connection with the area went back further than she'd thought. They returned to Doune, and continued onto the A84 towards Stirling, taking a right towards Thornhill. She'd never been there, and the views to the north were spectacular. Thornhill was a planned town, with one main street lined with neat little cottages whose front doors opened straight onto the pavement. At the first junction stood an odd, narrow, two-storey building, with a terracotta roof. Mac slowed as he took a sharp bend to the right.

Viv pointed. 'What do you think that building is?'

'At a guess I'd say it's the Lodge.'

'What? Masonic?'

'Don't sound so surprised. Crikey, Viv, you really are a townie.'

'What has my not knowing about a strange building, that I've never set my eyes on before, got to do with me being a townie or not?'

He glanced over to her and raised his eyebrows. 'Just sayin'.'

Mac and Viv almost had a history, and at times a frisson of sexual tension rippled between them. The ripple rose up her spine as she examined his strong profile.

He caught her stare, 'What?' He shook his head. 'I thought you'd have identified the hammer and sickle on the tower. It's a sure sign.'

Embarrassed at being caught gawking, she retorted, 'Oh, sorry not to be astute enough to "identify" an engraving at speed.' Her tone was more defensive than it should have been. She flushed.

But Mac either pretended he hadn't noticed or chose to ignore it. 'Ten miles an hour max.' His only retort.

Viv started to squirm. 'Who gives a . . . when a girl needs to pee?'

Mac glanced round. 'Seriously?'

'Yes, seriously. Any time in the last five minutes would be dandy.'

'There should be a loo open in the car park. Can you hold on?'

'Nope. Not an option. Pull over.'

This was no mean feat on the winding, up and down road. But with Viv wriggling in her seat Mac was under pressure.

'It'll have to be this farm track up ahead. There's no cover, though.'

Viv jumped out before he'd hauled the hand brake on. She left her passenger door wide open and pulled on the rear door handle. With both doors open she had a shield from both directions and crouched in her provisional shelter. Mac, ever the gent, whistled and became engrossed in the landscape opposite.

Seconds later she closed the back door, jumped in and grinned. 'There, that wasn't so bad, was it?'

Mac shook his head in disbelief. 'No She-wee in your bag then?'

She shook her head. 'How long 'til we get there?'

'Less than ten minutes. Not sure how they'll have it set up, but with darkness about to descend, I hope the team have taken the full kit, lights and all. Otherwise we'll have to get our torches out.'

They pulled into a car park on the edge of the lake. Trees sheltered a large gravel area and a small wooden building sat snugly at the base of a bank of earth. Viv wondered if it ever doubled as a campsite. They watched in dismay as the Historic Scotland boat pulled away from the jetty.

'Damn.' Mac tooted the horn. 'Jump out and we'll try and catch them.'

He tooted again and Viv bolted to the jetty with Mac close on her heels. He shouted, 'Ahoy!'

Viv got the giggles, seeing aspects of Mac that reminded her of Captain Pugwash, and that she'd never encounter when they were in town. But to her astonishment the skipper heard him and about turned.

Mac smirked. 'Not so crazy after all, eh?'

The boat drew alongside and the engine idled until Mac handed Viv in, before he joined her.

'Bit of an adventure. Certainly don't get to do much of this in our urban jungle.'

Viv, sensing that he was in his element, grinned and shook her head at his infectious glee.

'Thanks, mate. What are you taking over?'

The skipper, taciturn, shrugged and nodded at his cargo. Boxes of equipment and plastic containers with wires hanging out lay piled at the back of the boat, barely covered by a tarpaulin.

'I bet some of this is for the lights. They'll have taken a generator out already.'

Although this statement was directed at the skipper, he was reluctant to engage but gave a cursory nod in agreement.

Viv had never been to the Lake of Menteith, but knew it was famous for being the only lake in Scotland, a land of lochs and lochans. But also because of Inchmaholme, the small island at its middle, which had been home to a monastic community since the thirteenth century. The monks, an incredibly sociable bunch, had done lots of entertaining and it seemed that anybody who was anybody had visited. Robert the Bruce, more than once, attempted to woo the abbot, a fan of Edward I, and inevitably Mary Queen of Scots, having slept in almost every other bed in Scotland, had taken refuge there. Now all that existed on the island were the impressive remains of the old priory.

Viv stepped onto the quay and shivered; the wind had dropped but dampness had descended. She pulled her zip up as far as it would reach and drew in her chin.

Mac offered her a scarf from an inside pocket of his jacket. Gratefully, she wrapped it round her neck and tucked it in.

'Any idea which direction we should be heading in?'

The skipper indicated with his weather-beaten balding head.

'Cheers!' Mac said, before attempting to take Viv's elbow, which she duly shrugged off, as he led the way off the jetty.

The island was relatively luscious with mature specimen trees, remnants of shelterbelts, scattered round what remained of the buildings. Large gnarled rhodedendron bushes skirted the shoreline. Beyond and to the far left of the bushes they spotted a group of four men huddled round a hole in the ground. But when they approached they could see the men looked more like green-keepers, in their matching navy blue crested fleeces, than archaeologists.

Mac introduced himself and a look of confusion crossed their faces. He continued. 'We're looking for the archaeologists who've found the bones.'

The tallest of them said, 'I think you're at the wrong hole, mate.' The others laughed.

Then it was Viv and Mac's turn to look confused. 'What's so interesting about this one, then?'

'We've hit something metal, think it's a pipe.'

Mac nodded. 'So where is the other hole?'

Another, heavily-built bloke, sounding uninterested, said, 'At the chancel. Front of the nave.' Two of them laughed again.

The shortest guy said, 'Hard to miss them, though, with all their kit.'

Mac and Viv took off in the direction indicated.

Viv looked back and said, 'If I didn't know better I'd think we'd landed in a penal colony.'

Mac furrowed his brow.

'Those thugs looked as if they were in fancy dress or wearing those outfits for a bet. No way they'd seen a day's work.'

'D'you think?'

'Dah! Come on, Mac, with necks as thick as those I'd lay bets on them having bolts beneath their collars.'

'Christ! I thought I was suspicious.'

'Just sayin'.'

'Touché.' he said.

They soon found the other group hidden behind a church wall, cordoned off with blue and white crime tape.

As they approached Mac said, 'Why do you think that the skipper let us go in the wrong direction? Was that intentional?'

Viv didn't have a chance to answer before they reached the tape. Mac gestured to a PC for some bootees. From beyond the cordon a female police officer stepped away from a gathering of people looking as if they were prepared for bio-warfare, each wearing blue bootees and white coveralls with hoods. They shook hands and she introduced herself as DI Coulson. Mac didn't seem to know her so their exchange was formal. She explained that the archaeologists were there to record stone carvings, and one of them had noticed that a couple of the stones had recently been moved.

Mac crouched to examine the fringes of exposed earth. 'Some size of stone or what?'

The officer nodded. 'Yeah, it took those five guys,' she pointed to the group, 'with crow bars to lever it up.'

Viv interrupted. 'Is it just me, or shouldn't you expect to find bones beneath a grave slab?'

Mac and the DI looked at her.

Viv continued, 'So, what I mean is, they must have noticed more than a few disturbed tussocks.'

Coulson looked at Mac for permission to give more information.

Mac said, 'She's one of us. You're okay.'

Coulson continued. 'Well, there were tyre tracks. Which is really odd because the only vehicle on the island belongs to Historic Scotland's groundsmen. A small electric caddy, like a golf buggy. And it's not those tyres that made the tracks.'

'And the bones?'

'The grave contents had definitely been disturbed. And according to her,' she pointed to a slim dark-haired woman speaking to a group behind them, 'there are too many bones, Sir, and unless he was two headed . . .'

Mac looked intrigued.

The DI continued. 'There's one too many skulls for it just to be from the guy whose name is on the slab.'

'Were the archaeologists able to say who that was?'

'Yes, Sir, the grave isn't that old and belonged to . . .' she took out her pad to check the name, 'the Byron Ponsonby family. We now think that perhaps Sir and Lady Byron Ponsonby were both buried in there because another stone with her name on it lies further along the chancel.' She pointed to a smaller stone in the ground. 'And that's empty.'

Viv said, 'Often if the wife dies first she'll be buried in her own grave, until her husband dies, when they'll be interred together.' Viv recognised the name. The Byron Ponsonbys were a literary family, she'd only a couple of nights ago been flicking through a book that Sal had about local landed gentry, one of whom had been Sir Byron Ponsonby. He had earned the name of Don Giocasanova, and was a poet of sorts, which to Viv's mind was probably a euphemism for his being the family's naughty black sheep. He died in the nineteen thirties though, so why would he, and his wife, be buried on this little island at all when it had been gifted to the nation, by the Duke of Montrose, in the nineteen twenties?

Mac hadn't shown any recognition at the name but that needn't mean he wasn't aware of who the DI meant. Light was fading fast and the generator chugged into life, bringing with it enough illumination for a football pitch and enough noise for them to have to shout.

'Who is leading the dig?' Mac asked.

Coulson looked flustered. 'Sure. Sorry. Over here.' She led Mac and Viv over to the opposite side of the grave, where an archaeologist stood with his hands on his hips.

Mac produced a wallet with a laminated National Task Force

card, and held it up. The man squinted, and although there was no way he'd be able to read it in the glare of these lights, he nodded his assent that Mac was official.

They drew away from the din. Mac enquired, 'Have you sent anything away yet?'

The archaeologist was distracted. 'No. No, we haven't taken anything out. The grave is too new. We're only pawns in this. Bones are not what we're interested in.'

'Okay. So take me through how you found it, and exactly what you did when you discovered that the stone had been tampered with.'

'The thing is, lots of stones get moved one way or another, by grass cutting machinery, or if someone digs nearby the earth moves. The earth moves anyway, but with old gravestones tussocks of couch grass are often what secure their position. This one had not only been loosened but there was also a piece of sweetie wrapper. One of the team recognised a Snickers bar.' He pointed back to the grave. 'A tiny edge of it was sticking out from beneath the stone. It could only have got there if the stone had been lifted then dropped on it.'

'Did you bag it?' Mac eager to make sure that anything from the area was secured.

Coulson coughed. 'It's still in situ, Sir. Everything has been done by the book, Sir.'

'I'm not doubting you, Coulson, I'm just trying to build a picture. Besides, it's what happened before you arrived that we have to establish.'

Coulson nodded, reassured that Mac wasn't getting at her or her team.

Mac turned to Viv. 'Now why would someone take the trouble to open this monster sized grave? Surely to take something out? I don't imagine it was to put something in. But I could be wrong about that. Or what, to check if there was anything inside worth stealing?' He was obviously struck by something. He stared at Viv but she sensed he just needed a sounding board. 'This is another of those grey areas. Until we know whether something is missing or someone has left something behind, beyond the Snickers paper . . . but we can't know what, if anything, is missing until we know what was in it in the first place.' He turned to the DI. 'Could you find out from Historic Scotland if there are any family members who visit, or anyone else for that matter who comes to tend the grave? Are there ever any flowers left? Let's build up a picture of the Byron Ponsonbys who are still above ground, see if they have anything to tell us.'

Chapter Six

They were about to walk round the edge of the sacristy when Mac suddenly yelled, 'Watch out!' and pushed Viv so hard that she pitched forward and landed on her hands and knees. Mac wasn't so lucky. A piece of carved stone, the size of a bowling ball, toppling from a ridge above the chancel, narrowly missed his head. It caught him on the back and, winded, he fell to the floor.

Faster than she went down, Viv jumped up and motioned for everyone to stay back, 'Don't touch him . . . or the stone!'

She knelt beside Mac while he caught his breath. Viv beckoned to a female in overalls who bent under the tape and came to Mac's aid. He brushed her away and struggled to get to his knees. The white-gloved examiner checked the stone.

'It's hard to say, without getting up there, but it does look as if this has been worked recently.' She pointed to striations along one edge of the stone. 'These weren't made with the tools of a medieval stonemason. It's too late to take a look now, but we'll get up there in the morning and see what's what.'

Mac had managed to get to his feet but was doubled over, resting his hands on his thighs. The colour had drained from his face, and in this weird artificial light, his profile looked distorted.

'You okay?' Stupid question, but a start. 'You look like you'll need help to get back across the loch.'

He blew out a breath. 'I'll be fine in a minute.' But when he tried to straighten up it was clear that there was no way that within a minute he'd be any different.

The woman, who Viv assumed was the scene of crime manager, glanced over at Viv. 'I'll take a look at that.'

Mac started to protest but between them they soon persuaded Mac's jacket off his shoulders. Viv shook her head when she saw the mark on his back. The stone had caught his ribs and a horrendous swelling was already rising.

'There are bound to be broken ribs. You'll be lucky if that's all you get away with. We can't say for sure until it's x-rayed; you could have internal bleeding. Hope you're lucky.'

Mac whispered looking up at the female. 'Not feeling too lucky, Doc.' He had dropped to his knees again while they were freeing him from his jacket and with his head bowed he looked as if he was praying.

Viv, more worried now that she'd seen the damage, shook her head. 'Shit, Mac. We'll need to get you to A&E; it's not looking good at all.'

He tried to stand up again but agony was written all over his ashen face.

Viv spoke to the SOCO. 'You must have brought the proper kit to take a skeleton away from the site. Could we use that to get him over to the mainland?'

The woman nodded. 'Don't see why not. But will he agree?'

Mac interrupted them. 'I am here you know, and lucid. I got hit on the back not on the head. And I'm not going on any stretcher. Just give me time and I'll be okay to get back in the boat.'

Viv shook her head. He was as determined as she was. It would take all her powers of persuasion to talk him into A&E. If he wouldn't go, what was the best course of action? Could they make it back to the cottage? Sal had a fold-down bed in the cupboard under the stairs but he would probably insist on going home.

'Right, if we can get you back over the lake, I'll drive us back to Doune.'

She watched his effort as he struggled to his feet again and began to take baby steps in the direction of the jetty. Viv indicated with an outstretched pinky and thumb, to Coulson, who had already started to cordon off the area with blue and white tape, but began to punch in a number into her mobile, which Viv hoped was the boatman's.

It took a few minutes for her to get Mac sufficiently upright, and willing to lean on her, and at a snail's pace return to the shore. Viv heard an engine gunning and in hardly any time the boat was leaving the opposite side.

'Well done, Coulson,' she whispered.

As they waited, Viv tried to get Mac to continue leaning on her but he was having none of it. Suddenly he edged away from the jetty as the boat approached, and she heard him retching into the reeds.

Boarding a boat is an easy thing to do if you are in working order, but the minute there's a muscle out of place, or a broken bone or two, the whole stepping over a rail and down onto the deck becomes a drama. Viv looked at Mac's struggle and asked the boatman what the large lit-up building on the other side was.

'Lake Hotel,' he grunted, oblivious to Mac's pain, clearly grumpy about having to do an extra night run.

Viv snorted, 'Creative. . . Is there a jetty there?'

He looked at her with a furrowed brow. 'Yes, but . . .'

Viv nodded. 'Take us straight there. D'you know their number?'

He shook his head. 'You'll not need to worry about getting a bed. They're having a quiet season.' He coughed and wiped his mouth on his sleeve as the boat chugged away from the island toward the hotel.

The building they were approaching had an Edwardian edifice with a conservatory running the full length of the lakeside. It wasn't particularly beautiful, but it was substantial, and all Viv could think about was getting Mac space to lie down and with a bit of persuasion, strapped up.

The landing area was not so much a jetty as a series of dilapidated pallets. Viv panicked as they drew alongside because the drop was a couple of feet more than the one they'd left behind and that had been traumatic enough. Mac sat with his head in his hands, his breathing laboured and his pallor nowhere close to normal.

Viv rubbed his arm. 'Look, do you think you'll manage this?' She gestured to the wooden structure up ahead.

Mac turned and nodded. 'Not many options, have I?'

'We could take the boat back to the car park and offload you there. It would be easier than this. You'll have to jump here.'

'We'll give it a try. Don't look so worried, Viv, I'm not dead yet.'

Viv was worried. Mac was a big man. Tall, broad and solid muscle, she'd be of little help if he fell. His familiar aftershave mingled with his sweat and alerted her to the smell of her own anxiety. No one likes to be anxious or out of control. Viv hated that she was powerless to do anything for Mac. The boatman leapt off and attempted to tie up his craft, a wooden thirty-two footer, which he held with all his might as he looped the rope over a post sticking out of the loch.

The Lake of Menteith was one of Scotland's shallowest lochs and used to be a favourite venue for curling matches when it froze. The shoreline, a tangle of reeds, was impossible to walk through. Viv needed to get Mac right onto the shore. After a few minutes of pulling and much grunting, the boat was close and steady enough to disembark. Mac sat on the side of the boat, but with a line of tyres acting as buffers along the hull, he had to push himself off in order to clear them. Viv leapt onto the jetty, and pretended she would catch him if he stumbled. She almost felt his pain as he landed, grimacing, with his eyes screwed shut and jaw clenched.

He leant on her as they made their way to the front of the hotel. Viv pushed open heavy wooden doors and spotted a seat where she could park Mac. She went in search of a receptionist. Within five minutes she was back with a room key.

'They only have one room ready, but I reckoned with the condition you're in I'm pretty safe.'

'Yeah, but what about me?' He smiled, again more of a grimace than joyful, but Viv saw it as a positive sign.

She indicated which direction they were going in and set off along a corridor. 'I asked if they had a room on the ground floor and hey presto, all disabled rooms are on this floor, and still have views over the loch. Not that you'll be interested in views.' She turned to look back at him. 'Hope the beds are hard.'

'D'you think they'd have a first aid kit anywhere? It would help if we strapped up my ribs.'

'Once I get you settled I'll go and find out . . . Oh God, I must phone Brian and get him to see to Moll.'

The hotel was in the middle of an up-grade and there had only been two presentable bedrooms left, a single on the top floor, and the one that she was just about to enter. The room was standard size, en-suite with a shower and bath. Walls of pale grey made it gloomy and unwelcoming. Viv shuddered as she closed the door behind them. She switched on all the lamps. Mac sat on the bed with its charcoal and off-white covers. There was a tiny desk, a small tub chair and a window seat. A glass door led out onto a paved area where there were two white plastic seats upended over a tiny table. It was too dark to see anything beyond the end of the patio. Viv ran her hands down the heavy silk curtains then checked out the loo.

'Everything that you need for now is within ten paces. I'll be back in a jiff.'

Viv had been in difficult situations with Mac before, but she had always been the one who felt compromised. Mac had rescued her on a few occasions, but now that she was here she wasn't sure if she could share a room with him, no matter how injured he was. Her belly contracted. She thought she recognised the feeling but couldn't be absolutely sure.

The same guy that had checked them in managed to find a first aid kit. So she headed straight back to the room only to find Mac curled up, out for the count. She closed the door quietly, and began to remove her outdoor clothing: boots, jacket and Mac's scarf. She lingered, holding the scarf to her face, drawing in the smell of him; odd, no trace of cologne. She removed his boots and gently laid them one by one on the floor: dropping size elevens would be sure to wake him. His feet were enormous, but in fine black cashmere socks, they looked as if they were perfectly formed. She held his toes, an intimate gesture that sent a prickly sensation through her. She quickly pulled the duvet from the other side of the bed and folded it over him - weird seeing him so vulnerable. She stood with hands on her hips and glanced around the room, taking in its hideous decor. Deciding there wasn't much she could do, she retreated to the bathroom and sat on the edge of the bath. Piping hot water gushed from the tap as she tried to identify what the prickle was about.

Up to her chin in suds, she thought of all the people on the island who could have been injured by the falling rock. It was simple bad luck that Mac copped it; it could so easily have been her or anyone else who'd stood in that position. Or could it? How recently had someone been up there? Was it intended for an archaeologist? Or one of Coulson's team? Strange that it happened in the dark. She hoped these same questions would be in DI Coulson's mind right now. Could it have been one of Coulson's lot irked by NTF sticking their oar in? It was possible but unlikely.

She'd emptied another small bottle of Molton Brown's bath foam into the running stream, and now couldn't see any part of herself beneath the bubbles. She slipped under the surface of the water and held her breath. Luxuriating in the fact that there was endless hot water she turned the tap back on until her feet were poached. What would Sal say to the day's capers? Once her skin began to look, and feel, like orange peel she stepped out and wrapped an over-sized white towel round her body. Just as she reached for the smaller towel for her hair she heard a crash in the bedroom and ran through to find Mac bolt upright but confused on the edge of the bed. Glass shards were scattered over the floor by the door to the garden.

Viv backed into the bathroom, pulled on her trousers and shirt, then fumbled with her boots and jacket. She tried to open the now broken French door but the lock was jammed. She raced out of the bedroom door and down the corridor in the opposite direction to where reception was. She kicked open a fire door and stepped into the garden. She waited, listening, hair dripping onto her shoulders. She thought she heard a rustle from her right. A huge rhododendron bush stretched into the darkness and she followed the noise along its length, no idea where it would lead. Who or whatever it was kept moving but after a few minutes they were out of earshot. She stood still again and strained her ears, surprised at how many sounds echoed in the night air. A breeze sent a chill over her and, shivering, she about turned and retraced her steps to the room. The receptionist, jack-of-all-trades, was there with Mac who although standing to his full height was grimacing with pain. If you didn't know him you'd assume he was the aloof type.

'What d'you think happened, Sir?' The receptionist said, sounding marginally pissed off that there was action at all in this, normally anaesthetised area of the National Park.

Mac didn't answer but pointed to Viv who, still shivering, said, 'I've no idea what happened. He was asleep and I had just got out of the bath when I heard the sound of breaking glass. I ran through, didn't see anyone except . . . Mr Marconi sitting on the bed. The door to the outside was jammed, so I took off down the corridor and exited through a fire door at the far end. I heard someone . . . or something in the garden beyond the bush but couldn't see anything.'

The guy sucked air over his teeth. Not a good sign, Viv thought. Then he said what she'd predicted. 'I don't know if I'll be able to get maintenance in at this time of night and I've got no other rooms that you can use. I suppose I could put some cardboard over it.'

Viv looked at Mac struggling to hold himself upright. He said,

'It'll take too long to fix, we'll have to move on. But we'll be back in the morning to take a look round. Someone didn't want us to stay here. You think about anyone who might want the hotel empty . . . and of course, what you can reasonably charge us for the room for . . .'

Viv glanced at her watch. 'An hour.'

The poor guy had obviously never had to charge his rooms by the hour, and stood like a caricature, scratching his head, still doing the sucking air thing. Before she lost the plot, Viv got busy, grabbed her things and ushered Mac out to the reception area. She sighed ostentatiously, eyes reaching for her hairline at the inefficiency of the situation. No wonder the place was empty. If she owned the place . . . Blah, blah! She reminded herself that she didn't. The guy wandered behind them.

Viv asked, 'Could you get us a lift along the road to Historic Scotland's car park?'

'Sure, the barman isn't doing much.'

Viv looked round and noticed a rope across the bottom step with a sign reading 'Staff only'. She knew it hadn't been there earlier and wondered how, if she'd wanted to, she'd have accessed the single room on the top floor. Perhaps their intruder was a member of staff? She'd spotted a couple of unshaven guys at the bar; one of them looked like a younger, thinner version of the skipper. Again, she reminded herself that if you lived around here there were very few places to socialize and everyone was probably related in some way or other.

The monosyllabic barman dropped them at the Audi and as he drove off Viv stretched her hand out. 'Keys?'

Mac rooted around in his pockets and threw them to her, but immediately regretted the throw.

Viv bit her lip. 'I felt that.' She flashed him a cheeky grin. 'Something quite reassuring about having the upper hand. I must make the most of it, and stop thinking of you as my commissario.'

Mac grinned, 'I like the idea of you thinking of me, whatever the fantasy.'

Viv shook her head. 'You wish! Besides, it's not like you're capable of anything other than curling up and resting. Listen, we'll go straight to A&E and get you properly checked over.'

This time he didn't object.

The Audi was so different from her own car and she couldn't get the seat into the right position. Then as soon as she drove off she felt the car pulling to one side.

Viv stopped before they'd even hit the road, and got out. 'Mac. You stay where you are and I'll take a look.' She grabbed a torch from her bag and flashed it over the front wheel. 'Shit! That was not an accident.' The front tyre looked as if it had been shredded. Now there was no way that the earlier capers had been accidental.

Mac crossed his arms and laid them against the roof of the car. Then resting his head on them, barked, 'What the fuck is going on?' His voice, with a bit of energy behind it, sent a wave of reassurance over Viv.

'No idea, Mac, but if I didn't know better I'd think that

someone had it in for you. Got an angry ex hiding away somewhere that I don't know about?'

Viv walked to the back of the car and opened the boot. Unlike in her own car it was tidy, so access to the spare wheel was easy. Everything that she needed to change the tyre was neatly stored in its proper place. She hauled the temporary tyre out, laid it against the car and assembled the jack.

'I can do that.'

'Yeah, sure! You and whose army? You go and find somewhere to sit while I get this done. It should only take ten minutes.'

But Mac rolled the tyre to the front of the Audi. Then he checked all the other tyres before nodding to Viv. 'I was worried for a minute that we might fix this and then discover that the others had been ripped as well.' He blew out a breath of exasperation. 'Who would want to do this? And who would break a window and run away? I mean how juvenile is that? I don't get it, first the stone, which, by the way, could have landed on anyone at the site, then the smashed window, and now a slashed tyre. It's mad, totally mad.'

Viv was already lying on the ground trying to find the jack point with her torch. Once she'd located it she hiked the car up and loosened the wheel nuts, which took some doing because they'd obviously last been tightened by the A-Team. She heaved and heaved again, and eventually she managed to get them free. The rest of the job was easy, and as she'd predicted, only took ten minutes. 'By the way, if you think about it, each of these attacks were different, different motivations with different consequences. Okay, let's say the stone could be random. But breaking our window was specific, a sure sign that someone wanted us to move on. This,' she pointed at the wheel, 'contradicts the breaking of a window, 'cause it prevents us from going anywhere. Either there's something that we're both totally missing or the person behind this doesn't have a clue and is just pissed off with us. Doing stuff in the hope of annoying us.'

Mac nodded. 'Let's get going.'

Chapter Seven

Once on their way Viv looked at Mac. 'You done in?'

'Really sorry about all this, Viv. You're meant to be up here having a break. A well earned rest, and look what I've got you into.'

She patted his leg. 'I wouldn't have it any other way. Besides you didn't get out of bed this morning thinking, now what can I do to piss Viv off today, did you?'

He shook his head. 'I sure as hell did not, but if you hadn't come to Sheriffmuir with me you'd be tucked up in that cosy cottage with a book and Moll. My God. Moll, did you ring . . .'

'Relax. It's sorted. I phoned Brian and he's more than happy to go and check her. Although she'll be delighted to see us, I'm sure.'

Viv drove as slowly as she could get away with on the windy road back. After half an hour they had to make a choice between taking the fork to Stirling or continuing to the cottage. Within ten minutes they were entering the estate gates and bumping up the track.

Mac continued to argue his case. 'You know even if there are a couple of broken ribs there's nothing they can do about them. If you strap me up it will do just the same job.'

Viv was incredulous. 'Strap you up? You should be so lucky.' Then she grinned at him. 'Only kidding. Let's get you inside.

Nothing like a cup of tea to sort out the problems of the world. Then we can make a decision about what's best.'

Moll was already barking, and the security light on the porch flashed on as they slammed their car doors.

They both smiled and Mac said, 'Reassuring. I guess that's why people have dogs.'

'Yeah, that and the small but crucial fact that they never judge you. Unconditional love.'

'I can do that.'

Viv spun round to check whether he was kidding or not, but he looked serious. 'You don't honestly think that it's possible for a human to love unconditionally, do you?'

'Sure. Why not?'

She snorted. 'Because it's bollocks. We carry too much freight. We all have an agenda and distort our lens to make things fit what we want. Life's an emotional soup. No way you can separate your crap from the rest of the pot.'

'God, Viv, you're such a cynic.'

He edged himself down onto the sofa and groaned loudly, as Viv crouched on the floor fussing over Molly. 'What now? Tea!' Viv dusted off her thighs and straightened up. 'I'll get the kettle on. Feeling a bit peckish actually. So much for dinner at the Inn. I guess you're not hungry?'

'Not really. Tea and a biscuit would do me.'

After tea Viv asked Mac to strip his shirt off so that she could dress his wound. Sal's medicine cabinet came up with creams and bandages enough for an army. She smiled, wondering what Sal had had in mind when she'd bought such a huge first aid box. Viv had once cracked a rib playing tennis and had it strapped so she kind of knew what to do.

'Better straddle an upright chair so that your back is straight. And, here, just in case.' She handed him a couple of painkillers and watched with disgust as he popped and swallowed them dry.

'If they are broken this is going to hurt. So bite on this. Those things won't kick in immediately.'

She handed Mac a piece of folded cotton gauze.

'I won't need it.' But as soon as she tightened the bandage he yelped and tucked it into his mouth.

As Viv bandaged, Mac distracted himself by trying Coulson's mobile, but his call went straight to her answering service. He removed the lint from his mouth and turned awkwardly to look at Viv. 'In that chancel it would have been mighty difficult to get up there without anyone noticing. I mean the height of ladders it would take, never mind trekking over from the mainland with them . . . the boatman or those other guys we met must know something.' He sent Coulson a text. 'There's no way that they're ignorant of the grave . . . I was going to say robbers but we don't know if they took anything. Although they did leave something behind that they shouldn't have.' He took a deep breath and stared at her. 'I wonder if that was the point. Maybe they saw the grave as a good place for storage. What a caper . . . What did you think about Sheriffmuir?' He didn't wait for her to answer. 'I thought that woman was odd. Why do you think she took off?'

Viv waited, certain he just needed a sounding board again. But he raised his eyebrows in a query. 'Anyone home?'

'Sure, I think she might have had something on her mind, or something she wanted to hide from us. But a connection to the dig, I'm not so sure.'

'So you think she took off just for fun?'

'No, I'm saying I don't know why she took off. But if her family have been on that moor for generations, which by the way was the only thing that she seemed willing to give us, and with a touch of pride, she'll think of that land as her own. Doesn't matter who actually owns it. All her life she'll have played there and walked it. It must feel weird when people, strangers, come along and start digging it up. But before I get even more fanciful, maybe she had a dental appointment or something. Don't let's do that complex equivalence thing.'

He screwed up his face, 'Complex what?'

'You know, when something happens and you jump to the conclusion that it must be one thing, usually the worst case scenario, but it turns out to be perfectly simple, innocent . . . like a dental appointment and not an affair or a murder.' She smirked. 'It comes from NLP.'

He snorted, 'You and your psychobabble.'

'What would you do without it?' She grinned at him. 'You couldn't live without my insights; you have to admit psychobabble's had its uses.'

'I concede it has, but it still doesn't mean she was going to the dentist. Why didn't she come out and say hello, like any normal person, and tell us she was in a hurry? But no, she sneaks out to the barn, gets in her pick-up and takes off. Only stopping because I stepped in front of her. Call me suspicious but that did make me kind of suspicious.'

'Okay, okay, just sayin'.'

She helped him back into his shirt, then cleared the first aid kit away.

When she was in the kitchen she heard his phone beeping, but continued washing up before returning. 'Any news?'

'Yes. That was Coulson. The boatman has been given notice to retire and he doesn't want to. He's being difficult about a few things.'

'According to who?'

Mac shifted awkwardly in his seat. 'The Historic Scotland guys said he's been a pain in the arse. Making their lives difficult by not doing stuff that they need him to. One of those things is ferrying equipment like grass cutting replacements etc. etc.'

Viv shook her head. 'Nah, he didn't look fit enough to run away as quickly as the person that smashed the window. You heard him huffing and puffing trying to pull the boat against the pier . . . Or am I just being ageist? I can't see him up a ladder either. But that definitely is ageist. If Sal's aunt was anything to go by she was up clearing the rones 'til her nineties. Slashing tyres, anyone could do that, but I just can't see it. Okay, delete my comments about the boatman. But surely if you wanted to hang onto your job you'd do everything possible to keep them sweet. Make yourself indispensable.'

Mac nodded. 'What could he possibly have against me? I don't know him from a bar of soap . . . On another note, when you asked if I might be having difficulty with an ex I did wonder. I've had a few emails from . . . Oh, never mind, I'm being paranoid now.'

'Fuck off, you! Don't do that "Oh never mind" thing. It totally gets on my tits.'

He raised his eyebrows.

'Again. You wish! What sort of emails?'

'Nothing that I can't sort. Look I'd better get myself home . . .'

'Eh, I don't think so. There's a spare room.'

He looked appalled, 'No, no, I'd be better off in my own bed.'

'Okay, here's the deal. You can go home to your own bed, if I drive you. Leave your car here and I'll pick you up if you need transport.'

He was about to protest, but she shot him a look. 'Deal.'

Once inside her car she slipped out of the drive onto the lane, over the humpback bridge and up to the T-junction. 'Which way? I've no idea where we're going.'

'Sorry.' Mac shook his head. 'I wasn't thinking. Take a right. After five minutes on the main road he said, 'Left here.' They travelled for another ten minutes up onto the Braes of Doune before reaching a really rough track on the right. 'Up here.'

They stopped in the back of beyond, but when she got out of the car and looked back over the Carse of Stirling she couldn't believe how beautiful it was, with lights beneath the Castle and twinkles way into the distance. 'I bet on a clear day you can see a huge swathe of Scotland.' She turned to see him struggling with his key in the door. 'Watch out, I'll get that.'

The house, an old stone building with two storeys, was surrounded by rough ground with evidence of sheep right up to the front door. There was a wisp of smoke coming from the chimney, but overall the place looked pretty sad. Shabby paint on the windows and gutters were probably first on his to do list for this weekend.

He managed to get the key to behave and said, 'No probs. See, I can look after myself.' He bit his lip.

She smiled and shrugged. She'd got to do more for him than she'd expected. She'd done well to persuade him to let her drive.

'It's isolated.'

He nodded, ' That's why I've kept it. No one to bother me for miles. But great phone reception.' He pointed to a huge mast on the brow of the hill. 'You coming in?' He asked without conviction.

'No. No, I'll head back. But I'll see you in the morning. Ring me when you're up and about.'

Chapter Eight

Viv returned to Sal's cottage, ignored her own loud yawn, and booted up her laptop. She typed, 'Folklore of Stirlingshire' into Google and a whole bunch of wonderful tales about the area, including Sheriffmuir, turned up. She settled on the sofa with Moll's chin on her knees to read through them. The more she read the more wrapped up in them she became. The actual battle of Sheriffmuir in 1715 sounded like a shambles. The Earl of Mar allowed Argyll to retreat; consequently both sides claimed victory for a campaign that wasn't finished. She smiled. No texting in those days. She was attracted by names that she'd heard from Sal and read about in a couple of ancient books from the conservatory shelves. Viv had learned more about Sal from this cottage than Sal had ever let on. The man who carried the standard into battle was a staunch Jacobite, James Edmonstone. Viv remembered Sal saying that a cadet branch of the Edmonstone family once lived in the old tower house up the hill. She snorted at the polite use of 'cadet' – in other words, born on the wrong side of the bed sheets.

There were a number of sites on the Edmonstone family, but Viv was determined to contain her research to documents concerned with Sheriffmuir. She read on, until one story grabbed her attention; its title, 'Maggy O' the Bog'. How interesting that the woman on the smallholding had the same name. Family connection? Viv didn't believe in coincidence. Maggy, of the late eighteenth century, had made her name selling illicit booze to passing trade, but more specifically to soldiers who rode out to see her, from the garrison at Stirling Castle. The story implied that they didn't all make it back to their posts. Intrigued, she was tempted to ring Mac, but resisted – he needed to sleep. There was definitely a subtext, ambiguity about Maggy's real trade. Viv smiled as she reread it. She'd made her own illegal booze, and sold it to anyone who passed by, but the article also implied that the soldiers were looking for more than a flagon of ale. Was she responsible for their disappearance? Did she actually knock the soldiers off? And if she did, had they ended up in the bog?

There were two similar stories, as was often the case when oral traditions were finally written down. So she stood to go and print them off. Molly, blissed out after an extended ear massage, grunted at the upheaval. Viv laid the prints side by side on the table and scanned each for discrepancies. The first difference was the name, Maggy O' the Bog and the other was called Muckle Mary, but their stories were the same; each sold alcohol from an illicit still from a bothy on Sheriffmuir, and each had offered other services to passing trade and troops. Viv scratched her head. These were anecdotal stories collected in the mid-nineteenth century. The current Maggie O' the Bog must be related to this woman. Viv smiled at the notion of continuity in their family business; the woman today had been proud to mention how many generations had lived on the land.

Her final task was to have a quick look for the Byron Ponsonbys. There wasn't much to go on, although she did find one thing of interest − court proceedings about a land dispute. No house, but quite a few hectares at stake. Realising that she might have to collect Sal from the airport in the morning, she decided to call it a night. She opened the front door and called on Molly to go for her final pee. The clouds cleared to expose a half moon, and as in childhood she recited 'Hey diddle diddle' in her dad's memory.

Molly disappeared down the overgrown verge at the edge of the drive, which was unusual, and after a few minutes of her being out of sight, Viv called on her but her voice was absorbed by the dense bank of conifers on the left. Up to the right, through a copse of ancient oaks, she could see a single light burning in the tower. Perhaps the new tenants kept one on all night. She shivered and called again for Moll, but there was no sign of her trotting back up the drive. Viv stepped into her wellies and shrugged a jacket on before wandering out into the cold night air. An owl screeched in the distance and the Ardoch Burn was audible in the background. It was all too pastoral for her liking. She'd hardly gone fifty paces when she spotted Moll tucking into something, no doubt unmentionable, at the bottom of the track. Concerned about what she might wake up to if she didn't stop her, Viv bolted towards her. Before she reached her, a bulky, masked figure stepped out from the trees and tripped her up. She flew head over heels through the air and landed hard, with palms outstretched onto the muddy gravel. It took a second to recover herself, by which time the attacker had her pinned to the ground with one knee pressing into the small of her back. She yelped as he slammed a leather-gloved hand over her mouth. Moll, having finished snacking, started barking at the assailant. He struck out as Moll growled and bared her teeth.

Viv, no slacker in the fighting department, struggled to employ her usual tactics with his significant weight pressing down on her. She struggled and squirmed, eventually knocking her knuckles back into his face to connect with the bridge of his nose. As he yelped, he let go with one of his hands, giving her the chance to roll out from beneath him. Still on her knees, she aimed her elbow at his groin, only useful if she'd got the gender right. Her use of the knuckle punch was text book, but he jumped clear of her elbow. She thrust the heel of her hand back over her shoulder and jammed it hard beneath his chin, ramming it upwards until she heard a crunching sound. He squealed again and loosened his grip on Viv's mouth, just enough for her to sink her teeth into his bare wrist. He hissed through gritted teeth and Viv screamed a scream that should have woken the dead, but didn't. Still determined to keep a grip of her he grabbed a handful of her hair and held his arm across her throat. Moll, beside herself with distress, continued jumping and snapping as he kicked out at her. Viv, incensed that he'd dare to hurt Moll, with a surge of energy kicked her heel back into his shins and stamped on the arch of his foot. Suddenly, as if the attacker realized that his attempt was failing, he released Viv, pushed her hard onto her knees, and took off towards the old bridge leading to the village.

Viv stayed on the ground, catching her breath, with Moll jumping all over her like a crazy thing. 'It's okay, Moll. It's okay. Good girl. Good girl.'

With her heart racing, Viv got back to her feet, and stared in the direction of the attacker's footsteps. She stood, with hands on hips, and strained to listen for the echo of running steps or rustling, but heard neither since the wind was getting up and its gusts through the trees drowned all other noise. She about turned and walked back to the cottage, trembling as adrenaline pumped around her system. The dog weaved so close to Viv's legs she almost tripped her up. Viv collapsed onto the sofa and petted Moll. The wind buffeted against the windows and odd creaks made Viv tell herself not to get over-imaginative.

'What the hell was that about?' She grimaced. All day she'd assumed Mac was the target, but this was a good reason to believe otherwise. Was that falling stone aimed at her? The broken window didn't seem to be for either of them in particular, so it could also easily have been intended for her. The attack just now certainly hadn't targeted anyone else. Had they given the dog something that would distract her on the drive, knowing that Viv would go in search of her? Had her attacker known where she was at every step of her day? How could he? And more importantly why would he? Viv could think of many enemies who would go to these sorts of lengths in town, but not in the country, the twilight zone.

She locked up, double-checking each window and door with Moll by her side. Then slowly, listening for anything else to worry about, they took the stairs to bed. Viv stripped off and soaked her hands in a basin of warm water, picking the tiny bits of gravel out with tweezers, before returning to the bedroom where Molly was lying on the bed. Sal, a no-dogs-on-beds kind of woman, would have freaked out if she'd encountered the scene. Moll curled up on the white damask bed linen, with Viv's arm around her neck.

More relieved than she ought to be that Sal wasn't there to object, Viv lay in the dark with perceived enemies running before her eyes, as if her mind had become a cine-camera. It was difficult to narrow down those who would want to hurt her. Moll kept turning and scraping as if nesting. Then she stretched out, pushing her paws against Viv's side. Unable to settle, she jumped off the bed and scratched at the door. Viv sighed, but not entirely familiar with this dog's habits, thought it prudent to find out what she wanted. The dog trotted down stairs and pawed at the back door. Viv wasn't keen to open up, never mind let her out again, so she tried to comfort her in the conservatory. A gale was blowing, hammering rain against the roof, but Molly was having none of it and continued to scrape at the door. As Viv went to fetch boots and a jacket, she heard the dog vomit.

'Oh, my God. What have they done to you?' she mouthed in panic.

The dog continued to vomit, thankfully each time on a hard surface.

Viv remembered that Sal had left an emergency number. After going through the whole press this and press that thing she was becoming frantic, so that when a real vet answered Viv didn't allow him to finish his introduction. 'I have a dog who is continually vomiting. I think someone has tried to poison her.'

'What do the contents look like?'

Horrified, 'I'll go and see.' Viv put the phone down and scooped up some of the vomit in a piece of kitchen towel. 'It looks like, hard pieces of rabbit poo . . .'

'Well, that's good. It means the dog has brought them up before digestion. Could they be raisins or currants?'

'Yes. Yes, they could.' Viv pressed one between her thumb and forefinger. I think that's exactly what they are. What shall I do? Shall I bring her into the surgery?'

'The dog should be okay since . . . what's your address and the dog's name?'

Viv could hear him clicking on a keyboard. 'Molly. I'm looking after her for Sal Chapman.'

'Okay. I'm familiar with Molly, but let me just get her records up.'

Clicking again. Meantime Moll was off into the corner vomiting again.

'She's being sick again.'

'I think you'd better bring her in. If nothing else I can give her something to rehydrate her. Oh, and bring some of whatever she's throwing up with you.'

'Where exactly is the surgery?'

'Not far. Take the left turning past the info centre and keep left as if you're driving back on yourself. It's sign-posted. See you in five minutes.'

'Sure.'

Maybe this country thing wasn't so bad after all. In town chances of them knowing you and where you lived would be minimal. Viv put the kitchen roll loaded with yuck into a poly bag, swung a lead round Moll's neck, and ran out through the wind and torrential rain to the car. The dog resisted getting in. Viv wasn't taking any chances, so she lifted her onto the passenger seat and drove off. The sound of the engine and the splash of the tyres cut through the silence of the main street. When she turned into the tiny car park she was heartened to see the lights on and the door ajar.

The vet greeted Viv. 'Lucky I was here. I had to do a two-hourly check on a dog that had surgery this afternoon. Otherwise I'd have been in Dunblane.' He took Moll and she trotted amiably with him into a little room, where he lifted her onto a table and took her temperature. 'Her temperature is up. Let's have a look at the remains.'

Viv, screwing up her face, laid out the contents of the poly bag. 'I think someone left some meat or something with those in it. She wouldn't come back and she's not like that.'

'If her choice is between you and a steak, rest assured, it would take a mighty well-trained dog to choose you. However lovely you are.'

Was he coming on to her? She looked down at herself. Her jacket was flapping open exposing damp pjs clinging to her chest. She folded her jacket closer and said abruptly, 'Whatever it takes, make sure the dog's okay.'

He prodded Molly's belly and concluded that whatever had been in there wasn't there now. He gave her an injection to settle her gut. 'It's a good thing that she was sick so quickly. You wouldn't have wanted those,' he pointed to the raisins, 'to have gone into her system – those on their own are toxic to dogs. You'll have to keep an eye on her, but I'm guessing she'll be all right now that they're out. I'll give you something to pop into her water bowl.' He handed her a sachet. 'For the next twenty-four hours make sure she only drinks that.'

Viv lifted Moll off the table and didn't want to put her down. Mortified, she felt her eyes welling up, but managed to contain her emotion by flashing her credit card at him.

'Sal, er, Dr Chapman has an account. So we'll sort that out later.'

Viv hesitated, realising that Sal and this guy could possibly have had more than a professional relationship, so she wouldn't try to get away with not mentioning any of this. Since it was in the dog's interest to let her know, Viv conceded that to be upfront was best. She nodded her acceptance and carried Moll to the door, where the dog wriggled to be let down.

Back in the cottage Viv did exactly as the vet had told her, and emptied the sachet into a bowl of clean, luke-warm water before cleaning up the various piles of vomit. Her curses ripened as she followed Moll's trail round the kitchen and conservatory. They could have killed her. Who would be so cruel? It was one thing trying to get the better of another human being, but to attack a defenceless dog? That was entirely sick.

Once the floor was clean she made her way back up to the bedroom to find Moll already curled up on the duvet. Viv lay on her back, too angry to sleep and wanting to be close to the dog to watch for any developments.

Each creak in the house was amplified. She twitched and turned toward the slightest noise. She tied her hair up away from her ears, the better to hear the most minute movement. Country life was all very well, but there wasn't a neighbour like Ronnie, whose door she could tap on in an emergency. She watched and imagined that the curtain had moved, and got up to resecure the window. All the lights in the tower were on full blaze and the wind was showing no signs of giving up.

Chapter Nine

After what felt like only a few minutes of turbulent sleep she was woken by the ringtone of her mobile. She fumbled around the books, Swiss army knife, and photographs on the bedside cabinet, but too late, the caller hung up. Bleary eyed she checked the number. It was Jules, the editor that Viv wrote an occasional column for. When Viv had first been persuaded to do undercover work for a colleague of Mac's, her forays into journalism had been queried. They'd hoped she could be persuaded to take her eye off the story. But Viv knew that whatever 'they' said, 'they' already knew everything about her, from occupations to inside leg measurement, before they'd asked for her help. All the bumph about 'national security' was pure posturing. If she hadn't been cleared, she wouldn't be in the frame for any work at all, not even in their canteen.

She'd soon proved that indulging in a spot of investigative journalism was as good a cover as any, because people expected her to be nosey, intrigued, poking around. Since then she'd come up with the goods on more than one occasion. Besides, the buzz she'd got from the work, not to mention the bulging envelope that Ruddy the nameless front man had delivered from his invisible boss, was a heap more than she'd ever received for the odd column for Jules. And yet she was torn, deciding in the end not to ring back. Anyway, Jules was nothing if not persistent. If she needed Viv, there was no way she'd let her off the hook.

Viv padded through to the bathroom. A glance in the mirror made her recoil. Her reflection was like something from the house of horrors. Her attacker had gripped her face so tightly that she had bruises in the shape of his fingers on either side of her mouth. She rubbed them, hoping she'd missed patches of dirt the night before, but they didn't shift. Through the window, the eastern horizon was beginning to break up, and huge swatches of pink light filtered through the trees at the top of the hill. The gale had finally blown itself out. Viv reached for a dressing gown hanging on the back of the door, slipped into it, and went back into the bedroom to see Moll. She stroked the dog's ears and tried to chivvy her into a walk, but she showed no interest. She tried again, more enthusiastically, and this time the dog conceded. Together they retraced the steps of the previous night's debacle. Moll, on the lead, tried to return to the spot where she'd been snacking, but Viv pulled her in the opposite direction. There wasn't much to see apart from slight indentations in the gravel where she'd been scrapping and had scuffed the ground. Weird. A few trees had taken a beating from the wind and branches lay hither and thither across the drive.

If her hands weren't so sore, and her pride so dented, she could have convinced herself she'd dreamt the whole thing. But she ached, and the memory of going head over heels was not to be dislodged. In addition she clearly recalled the sheer bulk of the body that had landed on top of her. She was convinced her attacker was a man – he'd smelled blokeish, not quite Lynx but that kind of thing. Whoever he was he'd been fit, with taut muscles and the strength to lift Viv off her feet.

Moll was keen to return to the house so they wandered back inside and Viv put the kettle on, a reassuring habit that gave form to a day that was beginning too early. The light on the answering machine was blinking. Viv pressed Play.

Sal's voice echoed into the room. 'You'll never believe this but I'm still in Houston. There's apparently some sort of fire at an oil terminal and the runways are all closed. The wind is blowing smoke in the wrong direction. I'm going mad out here surrounded by Stetsons.'

Viv nipped upstairs, found her mobile by the bed, and rang Sal's mobile, but her voice mail kicked in. Viv went back to the answering machine to check what time the message had been left. Sal must have called when Viv had been driving Mac home last night. With all the shenanigans, it hadn't occurred to her to check the calls earlier. Struggling with the translation of time zones, she figured that Sal would either be in the air, or in a hotel bed in Texas.

With her tender palms clasped around a cup of industrial strength coffee, Viv sat at the kitchen table and reviewed the events of the last twenty-four hours. What in God's name was going on? Who could have followed her to Doune? Sal and Mac were the only people she could think of who knew she was coming to the area. Meeting Geraldine in the village yesterday had been a

75

fluke.

Viv recalled the look on Ger's face when she'd spotted her new man and made a mental note to contact her, but shook the notion out of her head. She had enough on her plate — what with stones toppling, windows breaking, and tyres being slashed, not to mention the attack in the middle of the night. She could let go of whatever was happening between Ger and her beau.

She washed her cup under the tap and stared out as dawn still struggled to rise above the trees at the end of the river park. At first reassured to hear Molly lapping at her water bowl, it didn't take long for her skin to crawl at the audacity and brutality of whoever had tried to hurt the dog.

She pulled on joggers and a sweat shirt and shouted, 'Moll, lead!' She grabbed her fleece and a jacket, and slipped into her boots. Tossing the car keys above her head she caught them, a sign of determination. Today was going to be a day for results.

'Right, Moll, in the back.' She opened the Rav's rear door and the dog leapt in. Viv was impressed at how quickly Moll had recovered. She cuddled the dog, who had grown in her estimation, for just being a dog and with relief that she hadn't anything worse to tell Sal. There was a lot to be said for pairing up with a dog. Moll's enthusiasm never waned, and she didn't baulk at Viv with bed-hair and unbrushed teeth. Viv breathed a huge sigh and drove off down the drive.

The views across the Carse on the Thornhill road as the sun rose were spectacular. A low lying mist hovered beneath the hills to the west but it looked as if it would clear and the blue strip above would take control of the sky. There wasn't much in the way of traffic. She tried the radio. Switched channels, but couldn't find anything that didn't feel intrusive. She pushed the off button. Moll had taken up her favourite position, in the back with her nose settled between the two front seats. Viv stroked her muzzle and the dog made suitably grateful noises. It seemed to take less time to get to the lake; daylight and that strange trick of familiarity had shortened the distance. Was perception the leader of the human dance? She decided to leave the car at the entrance to a forest track and walk through the wood so that Moll could get a bit of a run. Bad move. The extending lead kept catching on low branches as Moll swerved off the path to follow interesting scents and after ten or fifteen minutes Viv took Moll back to the Rav, and locked her in leaving a window open by six inches, and jogged back towards the lakeside car park. There wasn't any sign of life, and Historic Scotland's boat was tethered to the jetty.

The ticket hut had a window on the front and one on the side. She peered in at the side but the glass had a film of moss over it, which she didn't want to disturb, but prevented her from reading any of the sheets of paper on the desk. It took another five minutes to jog along the roadside to the hotel. The large car park was almost empty, with only a shabby pick-up and a grey transit van with a decorator's logo on the side parked by the back door. They were early to work. Or perhaps they hadn't gone home. Maybe those guys in the bar last night hadn't been locals and were tradesmen here to do the refurb. Viv reprimanded herself for making assumptions, then softened, given the circumstances. What with Mac in pain, the uncommunicative, recalcitrant boatman, then the ineffectual guy on reception, a girl could become overly critical. But whoa, that there was enough judgement to get her into hell. She reminded herself that everyone she met was fighting a battle that she knew nothing about. Go easy. So when she spotted the receptionist guy struggling to heave a huge black bag into an industrial bin at the back door – to what she supposed were the kitchens – she smiled and said to herself that he wasn't so bad.

Beyond the hotel, at the end of the car park, behind a bank of laurel bushes, she could make out a long, low, wooden building. Once the guy retreated into the hotel, she edged along a row of silver birch trees that shielded her from the road. Once behind the laurel she could see that there was smoke coming from a chimney at the end of the building nearest to her. Possibly staff accommodation. It was shabby, and reminded her of huts at Port Seton, where she'd had family holidays as a child. The sort of cheap chalets you'd find in most holiday camps, where wind and water-tight didn't matter so much when folks were out at the shows or the slot machines all day, and in the pub at night.

To get to the other end of the cabins she had to sneak behind them, which meant scrambling through a tightly planted conifer wood extending right up to the edge of the lake. There was no reprieve from scratching branches until she crawled free of them at the far end of the last cabin, the shoreline barely a metre away. The narrowest of gravel paths circumnavigated the building, but it was too risky to use it since smoke coming from the chimney was a sure sign of life. There were four doors at the front, each with a window looking out onto the laurels. Viv reflected, what with the dense conifers at the back and the laurels at the front, that the staff must suffer from SAD. Viv lived for big skies. The West Bow might be in the centre of a city but she had huge uninterrupted skies for one hundred and eighty degrees to the south, east and west.

Each section of the cabin roof had a metal flue sticking out. Probably a wood burner attached to each, but only one lit. She looked over to the island. It was enchanting, with mist suspended just above the lake and the ruins of the abbey creeping out over the top. She shivered, although there wasn't a breath of wind in the cloudless watery blue sky. With the way the trees reflected on the edges of the water it looked as if she could step out onto it.

The sound of a door opening startled her and she crouched into the end wall of the cabin. She peeked round the corner and, to her surprise, saw the boatman stoop and lock the cabin door. With his key secured in an inside pocket he waddled through a man-made break in the hedge towards the main building. Within a minute or two she heard the sound of an engine objecting to being woken up. Her shoulders dropped, and she asked herself why she was getting het up about having a look around? She reminded herself that this kind of thing was small fry compared to some of things she'd tackled in the last year. Taking the risk she ran along the path in front of the cabin windows and doors, and checked through the gap in the hedge to make sure he really was on his way. With relief, she watched as he reversed the mud-spattered pick-up and took off towards the ticket office and ferry car park.

She immediately rummaged in her inside jacket pockets and found latex gloves and her picks. What she thought she'd gain by breaking into the boatman's accommodation she'd no idea.

She blew into her cupped hands, trying to breathe life into fingers that were numb. The gloves took some persuasion to fit snugly but as soon as they did, it was an easy lock to pick. Nothing sophisticated for staff who wouldn't be expected to have much in the way of possessions. But once she stepped over the threshold she was heartened. What little furniture he had was quality stuff and, judging by the residual smell of almonds, had been lovingly polished. It was also, given the boatman's shabby demeanour, completely incongruous to see a couple of Victorian oil portraits hanging side by side above an equally incongruous nineteen-fifties fire surround. One was of a man in a grand military uniform, the other of a young woman in a cream silk dress with a lace bodice and one finger pointing towards the sky. Viv stared at the pointing finger knowing that it signified the woman's death. She assumed the paintings meant that his family hadn't always been simple boatmen.

There were two small rooms to the back, which could have been bedrooms, but only one had a bed, neatly made, with a threadbare but handmade quilt over the top. On either side of the bed stood a chest of drawers, both of deep mahogany with ornate brass handles, not cheap. The other room was used as a little library or study. She screwed up her eyes and scanned the shelves, trying to make out the titles, but the old, gilt spines were impossible to read in the gloomy half-light. Large picture books were mainly on natural history, flora and fauna. A small bureau stood beneath the window, facing out to the impenetrable wood, which blocked the light. A vintage typewriter, with a blank sheet of paper in its reel, sat begging to be used. She backed away from it before temptation to strike the keys got the better of her. A tall, narrow, wooden chest with slim drawers stood next to the door. No locks. She pulled open the first drawer and a sheet of paper with the familiar logo of the AA sat on top. She slid it out and checked the name. Edward B. Ponsonby. She whistled and looked at another couple of documents: one, public liability insurance for skippering a boat carrying passengers; another a demand for rent, both addressed to the same name. Now that was intriguing. So the grumpy boatman was a Byron Ponsonby. This shone a new light on the situation at the island. But what might be illuminated?

As she gently pushed the top drawer back she heard an odd shuffling noise – definitely something inside the house. There was nowhere for her to hide. She glanced at the fixing on the window. Not even she could squeeze through the six by twelve opening at the top, and the bottom pane was secured. She stood at the back of the door and held her breath. The noise ceased. She crept out into the sitting room but couldn't see anything. Then sticking her head round the only door she hadn't opened, the bathroom, she gasped. A pair of bulbous, yellowy green eyes stared out at her from a large cage fastened to the wall above the bath. An iguana, she guessed, but didn't stick around to ask it. Why did people have pets that they couldn't cuddle?

She left the front door as she'd found it, and edged back along the silver birches toward the road. She wondered about checking the back of the hotel, but thought she'd probably found their intimidator and broke into a jog, trying to shake off her adrenaline. A couple of cars slowed to avoid her on a bend. As she passed the car park for the ferry, she heard the purr of the boat's engine as it idled at the jetty, so stopped to watch as a couple of guys in navy blue Historic Scotland uniforms loaded up the craft with wayward rolls of drainage pipe. A benign scene, were it not for her new found knowledge – that the skipper had a vested interest in the island. She stood, concealed by a hawthorn bush, and waited until the boat chugged out onto the lake before making her way to the ticket office.

It was still closed but a woman in the same uniform as the guys who'd loaded the boat, and thick woollen fingerless gloves, said, 'The first crossing's not 'til ten.'

'Oh right, sorry. I was here yesterday and left my umbrella. I wondered if the boatman had handed it in?' The lie rolled smoothly from her tongue.

'Not likely, Eddie's . . . well, never mind. I'll take a look inside if you give me a minute.'

The woman tinkered with a couple of LPG tanks, protected by a cage at the side of the building. Once satisfied that their fittings were secure, she turned to look at Viv. 'Not exactly the ice-cream season yet, but the chiller has to be on just in case there's a delivery.'

She unlocked the cabin door and they both stepped inside. It was warmer in the car park and Viv shivered.

The woman noticed and said, 'You get used to it – at least it keeps the wind off.'

While the woman scouted around lifting boxes and poly bags, Viv tried to read what little paper there was lying on the desk.

The woman announced, 'There's no sign of an umbrella here. Sorry.'

'Has he been here long?'

The woman's eyebrows met in a quizzical response. 'Who? Has who been here long?'

Viv tried to sound as if she didn't care, and pointed to the ferry. 'The ferryman? I just wondered how long anyone could do a job like that. You know being mostly cold and wet, never getting to know anyone. People come and go. Passing ships in the night.' Viv was digging a hole that could be tricky to get out of. She should make a move.

The woman was busying herself extracting coins from plastic bags, the float for the till, and also stared out at the receding ferry with its gentle wake. 'Oh, Eddie's one of those guys who likes solitude. It's like dragging blood from a stone trying to get any conversation out of him. That's what comes from living on your own for so long.'

Viv nodded her agreement and backed out of the door. 'Thanks for looking for that brolly.'

She arrived back at the car within minutes. Molly, curled up on the driver's seat, stood, wagged her tail, stretched a beautiful down-dog posture across to the passenger side. Viv opened the door and couldn't decide who was happier to see the other. She squeezed herself in and Moll twirled back onto the passenger seat. Viv wondered about the implications of a real live Byron Ponsonby being on site, and the likelihood of him allowing anyone to disturb a family grave.

'Not likely.' Viv said aloud, and was rewarded with an enthusiastic sloppy lick from Moll.

Chapter Ten

During the return journey Viv's thoughts skipped around. First in amazement at how quickly she'd made a judgement about the boatman. It was easy to pigeon-hole others based on how they look and what they do for a living. Although, the boatman had done nothing to make anyone think that he could have a connection to the grave, so by omission he had actively constructed that image himself, intentionally excluding his aristocratic background. In a way Viv understood why he would do that; people always struggled with the fact that she was a hairdresser with a PhD, and when she'd added journalism to the mix, they were even more confused. We like neat boxes and if someone doesn't fit into one we're left at sea, or worse, suspicious. What would people make of her latest escapades? Not that she could talk about those.

She reflected on her own need for solitude, and the fact that her escape to Doune was to recover from an operation. Not the kind that involved scalpels or anaesthesia; more adventurous than that. It began one wet afternoon in an Edinburgh supermarket, while she stood testing the avocados, pressing the top of each one carefully so as not to bruise it, and a voice interrupted her mission.

An English, educated voice, subtly disguising a mother tongue, said, 'I think you'll find that applying pressure renders them inedible.'

Viv, intrigued by an accent more suited to a royal court in the nineteen fifties than the veg isle, swivelled to see a tall, slim man in a beautifully tailored, charcoal grey suit.

She'd furrowed her brow and replied, 'Like most things in life, if approached with tenderness no harm is done.' She turned away, hoping that that would be the end of it. But after she had selected her avocados, he remained in her peripheral vision. It clicked that he wasn't there to discuss fruit.

He continued using the accent that she was now convinced was not entirely natural to him, 'Did you happen to notice . . .?'

She interrupted him. 'The chap selling the *Big Issue*?'

The suited man raised his eyebrows. 'Was that a guess? Or are you as good as they say you are?'

Viv raised her own eyebrows. She'd been recruited by a man with a ruddy face who'd always dressed in tweed. She'd never heard his name or from whom he took his orders; she could only guess. But he'd smiled like Santa Claus, which was enough to pique her interest. She'd loved the generic metaphor that was 'The Home Office', and wondered if this immaculately suited man was one of Ruddy's. She also loved that 'they', always said 'they', as if everyone knew who 'they' were. Mac did it without even realising it.

She'd replied, 'I'm sure your interest in avocados is being tested, so what more can I do for you?'

He blinked at her directness, and shot an indiscreet glance over his shoulder.

'I wouldn't have asked if there'd been a risk.' She smiled, softening, guessing that he must be even newer to the job than she was. 'Unless of course the avocados are . . .' she lifted one from her basket, 'bugged.'

'We wondered if you might be free for dinner?' He'd shot his cuffs like a member of the royal family.

'His boots.' She smiled.

The Suit took a second to click.

Viv had continued, 'The boots were probably made in Eastern Europe, but my best guess would be Russia. Slightly too square on the toes. So last year. Not exactly sought as a Western fashion accessory, but designer in Eastern terms. Which would lead me to believe that we're not dealing with any sort of sophisticated group. If they were, they'd have bought in bulk from Top Man.'

And that was how her last assignment had begun. She couldn't think of an avocado without remembering that meeting. The Suit had turned out to be one of Ruddy's men, but to his evident distaste, he'd been seconded, another of those homogeneous words, whose meaning relied on who was using it. The Suit, she'd discovered over dinner, had been given a sideways move, and consequently, taken a while to warm to Viv's replacing him. He'd made the mistake of believing that her hairdressing career was the measure of her intelligence. Hadn't he heard of Pearl Harbor?

But others on the team – 'spooks', the term made her think of 'Casper the Friendly Ghost' – must soon have put him right, because he'd so visibly changed his attitude to her, and their joint reconnaissance outings were deemed a success, even though for the final two days of their last project, Viv had ended up incarcerated in a container, along with twenty-six other girls, without food, water, or a bucket. She'd had better times, and now, only ten days later, the memory of the stench was not yet consigned to her reptilian brain, and still clung to her palate.

Mac, who had either led or instigated most of the projects that she'd worked on before, hadn't been in on that assignment. Her debrief had been for one person's ears only, so Mac knew nothing of what had gone on and although he hadn't asked, she guessed he was itching to.

Viv's usual way of recovering was to throw herself back into creative work, but on this occasion, with a bit of persuasion from Sal, she'd decided to try a bit of R&R. The week off had coincided with a forensic conference in Houston, which led to the offer of Sal's cottage in Doune. But Viv was finding R&R much more challenging than investigating, so, although she loved to sit with her head in a good book, there was no question of doing that if she could be out in the field throwing in her tuppence-worth with Mac.

Once back at Sal's cottage, Viv jumped into the shower, her mind busy with what she'd discovered. Breakfast was a slow, measured affair during which she made a commitment to a bowl of muesli. She stared out at the drive and wondered if by any chance someone up at the tower had seen or heard anything of last night's commotion. Worth asking? She unhooked a jacket and slipped out through the tack room. There was a narrow, overgrown path leading off Sal's drive, up a steep bank to the tower. She'd never been up this way and imagined that at some point the cottage had been home to a member of the household staff. She visualised some poor sod trudging between the tower and the cottage, leaving before sunrise and returning after sunset. Long days of pandering to the Laird. Once she reached the top of the hill she could see that the house was set in a courtyard created by high walls reaching out from a row of barns on one side, and the round end of the tower at the other. Part of the garden could be seen through an ornate fence, leaded into the top of a stone wall directly in front of the middle section of the house. There was access into the building by a few steps down and through a heavy studded wooden door. A tall gate set into the wall on the right-hand side was her only means of access, if she wasn't to walk the whole perimeter of the property. The gate creaked and she stepped through it onto a precariously slippery, moss-covered flagstone. She pulled the gate behind her, minding the notice on it to beware of the rabbits. She assumed it meant to stop rabbits from getting in rather than getting out. There were still lots of lights on but no sign of anyone around.

The barns had been converted into an annexe for the house. She thought she saw movement in one of the downstairs windows but it could have been a trick of the light as the sun occasionally crept out from behind heavy clouds. She knocked on the studded door but the noise echoed into a lifeless space. She wandered round to the back of the annexe and again thought she caught a movement, this time in the glasshouse at the far end of the garden. Was she losing her marbles? She stopped and scratched her head, staring into the spaces between last year's vines. There was no one there. Another gate, on the far west wall, led to a vegetable garden, but there was nothing much happening there. Adjacent to the carefully manured raised beds lay a young orchard, small trees with tiny buds on them, but no one doing any work. Viv was about to make her way back to the entrance when she heard a fit of coughing on the other side of the wall. She called out 'hello' but no one answered. She marched back across the lawn, out through the gate she'd entered by, and round to what she guessed would be called the back of the house. This side had all the evidence of the workings of the house. A long lean-to up against the highest section of the garden wall held all sorts of machinery and at the far end she spotted a man in immaculate John Deere overalls leaning into the engine of a ride-on mower. She called out again, not wanting to alarm him, but still got no answer. Was he wilfully ignoring her? She trotted over and tapped him on the shoulder; he almost leapt out of his skin. Yanking out his micro-earphones, he looked as if he was about to give her what for when the sound of an engine on the drive made them both turn. A white transit van stopped, executed a smart turn, and shot back through the gates onto the main road.

Viv and the guy stood for a moment. He turned to her. 'Now what can I do for you?'

'I was hoping to speak to someone from the house.' She pointed with her thumb to the tower. 'I'm not getting any answer at the door.'

'I'm only here on a contract. Once a year this thing gits serviced whether it needs it or no.' He smiled slightly. 'Money fur old rope. I think their gairdner brings his ane wheels.' He nodded to the shiny bodywork and engine in showroom condition. 'I clean the plugs an' that. Then they git sent a bill.'

Viv stifled a yawn. 'So do you know if anyone's around?'

'Not that ah've saw. Although the hens are oot so ah expect someone's been aroond.' He gestured to a large shed surrounded by chicken wire.

Viv remembered that Brian looked after the hens and decided that he was her best bet for information about the tenants from the tower. She about turned and walked back towards the grass path to the cottages. Just before she turned out of sight the mechanic shouted, 'A car wis drivin' oot as ah wis comin' in this morning. They werenae too keen to shut those big Victorian gates behind them. Ah had to go doon and do it so's the hens wouldnae escape.' He shook his head.

'What kind of car was it? And what colour?'

'Ah cannae mind. Japanese maybe, they all look the same these days. But it wis black.' When Viv shook her head at his lack of clarity, he said, 'Ah'm more of a trail bike man mahsel'.'

She nodded. 'Thanks.' And strode down to the cottage thinking why would anyone sit in their car all night when they could have taken off in the dark without being seen? It didn't add up.

Molly unsubtly nosed her bowl around the floor. Viv scooped

up the bowl, put a tiny amount of food in it, apologising for her neglect, and laid it on the floor. But instead of eating Moll started to bark and bolted through to the front door. Viv, assuming it would be Brian or the postie, was surprised to see Mac's bulky outline silhouetted through the window to the porch.

She swung back the door, 'How the heck did you get down here?'

He pointed a forefinger at her. 'Ways and means, ways and means . . . hitched with the farmer to the main road. He took pity on me and asked where I was heading. He brought me along to the end of the lane. He's got a huge piece of kit.' Mac enthusiastically spread his arms, but his injury forced him to drop them as quickly as he'd raised them. 'The wheels are taller than me and wider.'

Viv sniggered at his enthusiasm. 'Am I sensing a touch of mine's-bigger-than-yours, going on here?' She wiped her mouth, suddenly conscious of stray bits of muesli. 'How are the ribs?'

'Better than they were last night. I took more painkillers and knocked myself out. I thought if I got a good night's sleep I'd be cured. And here I am, not quite cured but much better, thanks to your ministrations.'

'There's coffee in the pot if you'd like some. I'd better get dressed.' As she edged out of the kitchen door she threw over her shoulder, 'Have I got a story or two for you!'

'Oi, that's not fair. I want the story before you go upstairs and spend twenty minutes on titivation.'

Viv stuck her head back round the door. 'Since when did you

know me to spend twenty minutes on anything?'

She left him in the kitchen nursing a cup of strong coffee.

Back within five minutes, she filled the kettle again and sat opposite him exposing her scuffed hands on the table.

'What have you been up to?'

'I was in a fight.'

Mac's face registered shock but he kept his tone light. 'What? I leave you for five minutes and you're off fighting the locals.' He smiled but it wasn't a happy smile. He stared over the top of his cup. 'Spill.'

'When I got back last night I went online to do a bit of research, which always takes longer than you think. Then after too many distractions way into the wee small hours I took Moll out and she wouldn't come back. I walked down the drive to see what she was up to and someone pushed me, and I mean really pushed me. I hit the deck, but as you do, I tried to get to my feet again. But he was on top of me, he weighed a frickin' ton, and we scrapped on the ground for a bit . . . Thank God for Moll, 'cause she launched at him, snarling and barking until he went to kick her, when natch . . . I lost it. I managed a few serious whacks but nothing that would leave him too badly injured . . . apart from a bite.'

Mac looked incredulous. 'So this puts a whole new light on the earlier attacks. Let me think this through.' He worried at a small nick on his newly shaved chin. 'So the toppling stone was more likely to have been for you? . . . That is, if it wasn't a complete accident, which neither of us believes, along with the broken window of our room.'

Viv bristled at the 'our'. 'The *only* room at the inn, if you don't mind.'

Mac raised his eyes to the ceiling. 'Jeez! Touchy or what? I wasn't accusing you of anything. I was stating a fact. Now, where was I before your paranoia jumped down my throat? Oh yes. Then you get into a brawl in the middle of the night. You said Moll ate something on the drive . . . d'you think whoever attacked you brought that something with him?' Before she could answer he stood. 'Let's go and take a look.'

She hesitated. 'I've already been out. I couldn't see anything, but yes they could have.'

'C'mon, let's go see. Two sets of eyes are better than one.'

Once Mac was convinced that there was nothing more to see immediately outside, he suggested they check out the old mill yard on the other side of the crumbling estate wall. The mill, now a ruin, had outbuildings that were used by Historic Scotland to repair and conserve stone for Doune Castle's curtain wall. To get access they had to walk to the bottom of the lane and turn back on themselves before climbing a post and rail gate; poor protection for the yard.

It was Saturday morning on a holiday weekend and the yard was deserted. At its entrance tarmac gave way to a sandy gravel surface. They both spotted the tyre tracks at exactly the same moment. There had been torrential rain the night before so any tracks were bound to be new.

Viv cleared a tickle in her throat. 'You thinking what I'm

thinking? They left a car in here? Get this. The padlock's missing.' She pulled a chain from round the gatepost and held it up. 'But why is the gate closed at all? If they crept out of here in the middle of the night, they surely wouldn't take the risk of stopping and closing the gate neatly behind them. It doesn't make sense. If only I'd thought to come in here after the attack.'

'I'm glad you didn't. But did you hear anything like an engine start up?'

'No. Nothing. And I lay awake for a long time, shame gnawing away at my brain.'

He frowned. 'Shame? What have you got to be ashamed of? He attacked you, remember.'

'Yes, but it took me too long to put into action all the self-defence I've learned at . . .' Her voice tailed off. 'It should be second nature by now.'

Mac rubbed her arm and didn't remove his hand. 'You don't have to be super-woman all the time, Viv.'

Unsettled by his gentle tone and affectionate touch, she uncurled her arm and slipped through the gate. She kicked around in the grass where Molly had been, but couldn't see anything. 'They might have had a key to that padlock.' Byron Ponsonby leapt to mind. 'By the way I had a quick look at the hotel this morning.' She turned to see him standing with his mouth open. She smiled and continued. 'It turns out our scruffy boatman is a Byron Ponsonby.'

'What? How do you know that?'

'Probably best not ask too many questions, but the woman in the ticket office more or less confirmed it.'

'Well, that puts a spin on things.' He shook his head. 'I'll need to have a chat with him, or get Coulson to. Let's go inside and I'll fill you in on what I got from her.'

Still distracted, she nibbled on her lip and nodded to herself. 'It could have been a hybrid.'

He looked at her in confusion. 'What?'

'If there was a car in that yard,' she pointed over his shoulder, 'I would have heard it leave. I wasn't remotely sleepy. But I never heard anything. There's no way a car with an ordinary engine could have moved without me hearing it. It had to be electric, a hybrid.'

'Good call. They are totally silent. One of the guys in CID has one, and he could easily take you out while he was reversing in the car park at Fettes.' He nodded enthusiastically. 'No probs.'

'Well, the boatman doesn't have a hybrid, that's for sure. He drives a manky old pick-up. But I've made a mistake about him already and I wouldn't want to go there again. He's defo worth another check. What does he have to gain by poking about in that grave? Or, what does someone else have to gain by setting him up?' She nodded emphatically. 'Yep, we'd better keep an eye on him and the other guys he works with . . . So who do I know with a hybrid?' She couldn't imagine. One of Viv's hair clients had one, but he, or rather, they, were on a cruise at the moment. Besides, they were so adorable, there was no way it would be them.

Mac's phone rang before they reached the cottage and he stopped to take the call. Once he'd finished he said, 'That was Coulson. There's nothing in the grave on Inchmaholme. Well, nothing that isn't meant to be there.'

Viv didn't get it. 'So how could we find out what *was* supposed to be in there? You surely weren't dragged over there on false pretences? . . . On purpose d'you think?'

He smiled at her. 'Lots of questions just waiting to be answered, Viv. First thing I'll do is find out who put the call through to ask me to go check out the island. Someone knows what's going on. But one thing's for sure, they were intent on getting me there. Unless it was someone at the Sheriffmuir site, they'd have had no idea you'd be with me. Which means the attack on you could be a separate incident.'

'By the way, I had a look online for the Byron Ponsonbys. The only thing I came up with that's current is a land dispute. But now that our skipper is in the frame things could be a whole lot different.'

'Worth a closer look.'

Once inside, Viv noticed the answering machine blinking, and reminded to try Sal again, rang her mobile but still got no reply.

'You couldn't stretch to giving me a few more painkillers?'

She looked at him and noticed that the bloom he'd arrived with had faded. 'Sure. I'll just get them. We could still get those ribs checked out. It's not too late.'

He brushed the suggestion away with an elegant hand. 'No. I'd rather milk being a martyr.' He threw her a grin. 'Too much to do. Coulson won't need us to do anything there, but I've had another message to say that they've managed to get what looks like another skeleton, or bits of, out of the ground. The rain yesterday washed away loads of the peat that was holding them together. So much for their tents. Anyway water rises in a peatbog. We could go back up to Sheriffmuir . . .'

She stared through him, her focus elsewhere, until he clicked his fingers. 'Hello? Anyone home?'

She shook her head. 'I was just thinking about Sal. She's due back today, I thought this morning, but I can't get hold of her. I'd like to pick her up from the airport and I wouldn't want to keep her waiting. Suppose we could go in two cars if you're able to drive.'

'I'm fine to drive. You don't have to come. I just thought . . .'

'No, no, I'm interested.' She interrupted him. 'It's just that I've got something niggling me about the attacker. I'm sure it was a man, because of weight and size.' She decided against giving him any further details. 'In the NLP world we're encouraged to ask what else could this mean, and what someone has to believe in order to attack another person. Attacks are rarely random.' Viv needed to find out what her attacker's motivation was.

Mac looked intrigued. 'Okay. Let's take the toppling stone. What else could that mean?'

'Well it could have been accidental and we were unlucky. Perhaps the mason just didn't stabilize it well enough, or he forgot to. Or it was meant for someone else? Mistaken identity?'

'Okay. Fair enough. What about the broken window at the hotel?'

She smiled at him, knowing that he'd avoided saying 'our' room. 'A passing hooligan, another case of mistaken identity, or someone pissed off that we were sharing a room? My money's on the boatman.'

'Okay, but surely he didn't have anything to do with the attack on you here?'

'Perhaps we're dealing with two different people. It can't be same old, same old, aggrieved lover, colleague, or other. They'd have to believe that I'd done something wrong. That I'd hurt them really badly. Perhaps I've stolen the object of their desire. Or perhaps I've stopped them from getting a promotion. Whoever it is believes that I am a baddie and if I am warned off, or worse, their chances would improve.' She rubbed her hands over her face and blew out a breath. 'The improvement to their lives would have to be pretty damn dramatic for them to lurk about in the middle of the night in the hope that I'd take the dog out again. Remember, Brian had already taken her out. So they couldn't be sure that I'd be out there anytime soon.' Then something occurred to her . . . 'Your car doesn't have a tracker on it by any chance?' This was a shot in the dark but worth checking now that she'd thought of it.

Mac looked alarmed. 'Not that I know of. But we could take a look.'

She also wondered about her own car but didn't say. 'You sit where you are and I'll go check. Are those painkillers kicking in again?'

Mac was in no fit state to roll about on the ground just yet. 'Yes they have . . . b . . .'

'No buts.'

Viv skipped back out to Mac's car and slid beneath it on the damp gravel. The microchips that they used for tracking these days were much smaller than they used to be. Like the mobile phone everything was shrinking. She focused her torch into the crevices and corners, as her training had taught her, but she couldn't see anything. As a second thought she opened the bonnet and scanned around the obsessively clean engine. There was something behind the battery but she couldn't reach it. There was also a strange smell, not oil or brake fluid but something odd. Probably just newness.

'Mac!' She shouted, but she needn't have as he was standing in the doorway chuckling at the sight of her struggling over the edge of the bonnet. 'Get over here. I think there's something.' Mac stood six feet four inches with arms in proportion, but his hands were unusually slim. He stretched down the side of the engine and fiddled with whatever was there, but couldn't get his forearm far enough down. He slipped his jacket off, handed it to Viv, rolled up his shirtsleeves, and tried again, first with one arm, then the other.

Eventually, as Viv's patience was waning, he pulled out a small cube with a tiny but powerful magnet on one side and inspected it carefully, wiping its surfaces. 'I don't think it's one of ours . . . But I'll check, find out who produces this, and hopefully who buys from them. Interesting, though. We, you or I are certainly the subject of someone's attention.'

'Is there any way you can disarm it so that they can't continue to locate us?'

'There is, but it might be useful if we let them carry on following us. We could trace the source, but we can only do that if the tracker is live. Let's get a quick look under your bonnet.'

Nothing there.

Viv pushed her hands into her trouser pockets, amazed that someone had been tampering with his car. 'You'd better get washed up. I've got Swarfega in my car.'

'It's not that bad. I'll be fine with soap and water.' He shook his hands as if they were already wet.

Mac wandered into the conservatory and spoke to someone on the phone. Viv heard him describe the cube, then say he'd send a photograph and ask them to do a check on any like it. He gave them details that she hadn't noticed and ticked herself off for not paying enough attention. She mused at how easy it was to forget that Mac did a tricky job because he had the nous to, not because he was a nice guy.

Mac returned to the kitchen. 'Okay. That's that done. They'll get a list from the suppliers.'

The ubiquitous 'they' reminded Viv that although she was now his colleague, there were still areas that she didn't have clearance for. She had no idea who he'd spoken to, but imagined a department somewhere in the bunker-like basement at Fettes whose job it was to find out stuff like that.

Mac attempted to rest his hands on his hips but grimaced and let them fall to his sides. 'Look, Viv, I'm happy to go back to Sheriffmuir on my own. You want to get things sorted for Sal. I'll ring you later and fill you in.'

'You not worried for my safety then?'

'Yeah, actually I am. I'll get hold of Mike Coates' lot. In fact I'll see him at the site and tell him. He'll get a presence down this way.'

'I'm not worried about them coming back. While I'm indoors Moll is as good an early warning system as any.'

'She wasn't last night.' Viv watched as Mac digested his own words. 'They must have given her raw meat. There's no way she'd ignore someone's presence on the drive, or along the wall, and certainly not in the middle of the night.'

'But after the attack she'll see them as foes, smell them a mile off. Don't fret, Mac. I'll be fine.' But he was fretting. She continued. 'Look, I have things to do. There's no food in the house, I'd like to comb through my laptop, check my mail for the last couple of months. I could have missed something that's gone into spam. In fact, we should both be vigilant about all our recent correspondence. If there's an identifiable enemy out there . . . No. They'd do everything possible to surprise us . . . I wonder how much actual mail is gathering behind the door of my flat? When I'm away Ronnie takes it up and puts it through the letterbox. Never mind me. I'm thinking out loud.'

'Sure, I'll check all my spam Viv, but I get so much crap, not exactly hate mail, but minor threats all over the place . . . You're right, though, we should both check. I wonder if it would help if we swapped laptops . . . I stop seeing stuff. I could easily have missed it.'

'Not a chance. What? Have you been scanning through my correspondence? I don't think so, matey.'

'Got something to hide? Too much lovey-dovey stuff?' He grinned.

Viv tossed a cushion at him. 'No, I've just got more netiquette than you.'

Mac awkwardly dodged the missile and walked towards the front door with his arm up, guarding his head. 'Mind, I'm walking wounded.'

Viv clapped her hand over her mouth. 'OMG, I'm sorry, I forgot.'

'No worries. Right, I'll head up to the dig while you do your stuff. I'm guessing if Sal gets back you'd like a cosy dinner for two?'

The idea made Viv's belly clench. 'No. Don't be daft. Come and eat with us. Sal will be jet-lagged anyway. If you don't hear from me, come round at seven and we'll swap what we've got, if anything. I'll do pasta.'

Chapter Eleven

Viv watched as Mac slowly manoeuvred his car out of its tight space. She stood gripping her upper arms until his tail-lights had entirely receded, and wondered where to start. Decision made, she tried Sal's number. Still no answer. She checked the fridge. Nothing much. A trip to the village was in order if she was going to cook for three.

Within half an hour she'd returned from the post office, which in Doune was a euphemism for a shop that sold everything you've ever needed, including the ingredients for carbonara and a salad - a high-risk meal, since Mac's parents were Italian and excellent cooks, a talent which he had inherited. She chewed the inside of her cheek, recalling all the delicious meals he'd cooked her, then thought, beggars and all that.

She was about to settle down with her laptop when her phone buzzed. An empty text from an unfamiliar number stared back at her. Viv was pretty careful about who she gave her details to, and in the circumstances couldn't just give this up as a wrong number. She'd get Mac to run it through a check later. She sighed and began scrolling emails from three months back. Whoever was threatening her, if it really was her, would surely be cooking up their next efforts by now.

Her spam was bursting at the seams with promos for anything

from high protein drinks to penile extensions. Viv snorted, murmuring to herself, 'What you get for having an androgenous name.' She couldn't find any emails that were remotely threatening. Her inbox was much the same, although there were one or two that she should have answered, and hadn't yet. She marked them as unread and kept scrolling.

Her phone rang and she answered it, still distracted by the screen. Sal's exasperated voice gave her a reality check. 'Hi, Viv, it's me. I'm in Heathrow, hoping to board any minute. I'll take a train to Dunblane and a cab up to Doune.'

'No way! I'll get in the car and by the time you touch down I'll be waiting.'

'No, Viv. I'm going into HQ. I want to have something checked.'

'Okay. I'll come into Fettes and get you.'

'Don't be daft. I'll beg a lift from Mac . . .'

Viv interrupted, 'Mac's already up here.'

Sal hesitated. 'He is? . . . Well, I can take a train to Dunblane and you can pick me up from the station. I don't know how long it'll take at Fettes.'

'Is something wrong?'

Another hesitation made Viv sit up. 'What is it, Sal?'

'I'm not sure if it's anything, but I've had a few dodgy emails and I thought I'd get the guys to look at their source. And they can't unless they've got my phone and my laptop. If I do it now it means I can relax for what's left of the weekend. I'll not be long.'

'But you know that I could do that.' Viv heard the echoing voice of an airport tannoy in the background.

'I'll have to go. I'll ring you when I get to Fettes.'

Viv knew that there must be something more going on for Sal if she wanted to get the Fettes guys involved, and felt panic rise that Sal mightn't be safe even to travel on the flight from Heathrow to Edinburgh.

She rang Mac. 'Hey. I've just had a call from Sal. She's on her way up from London and wanted to go straight to Fettes with her phone and laptop. Said she'd had some dodgy emails or something, but if that was all that was wrong she'd have let me take a look at them.'

Mac interrupted. 'Slow down, Viv. She's doing the right thing.' He sniffed. 'Wonder what it is? She's not daft. She must realize it needs something from the cyber team.'

'Excuse me! I'm the frickin' cyber team, remember? When they fail you come to me, so why doesn't she let me take a look at it? She won't get anything from them that she couldn't get from me and . . .'

'Whoa! There could be. But there's little point in speculating, or falling out over it until we know a bit more. When is she getting in?'

'She was boarding, but I don't know who she's flying with.'

She typed Edinburgh airport into Google and clicked on Arrivals and Departures. It didn't really matter which carrier Sal was flying with, the flight took under an hour so she'd be landing in about fifty minutes.

'What are you doing?'

'Checking the arrivals. I'll head down now. I'll keep you posted.' She cut the call. She knew that mentioning the emails was the way to get Mac to alert the cyber guys in his unit so they'd be ready and waiting. But if she could get a look first she had ways and means that would be a last resort for them.

It struck her that the stuff she and Mac had been experiencing might be to do with Sal and not them. It made sense, since Viv hadn't found a shred of anything in her own emails. Now Sal as a target would be a different ball-game altogether. As a profiler Sal had worked on some really ugly stuff in the last few years. Viv had learned a great deal from her, and understood how that kind of work put Sal in the firing line of some total psychos. Luckily most of them were doing time, but the odd one could easily have got out with a tale of good behaviour. Sal wouldn't forget any face and working someone's profile didn't leave too many stones unturned. There would be nothing she didn't know, from scars to the type of fillings in their molars. Information was currency, a unique power, which definitely opened Sally-Ann Chapman up to threats.

It occurred to Viv that since Sal was almost on home soil she could be at more risk. She grabbed her rucksack, keys and phone, and was about to jump into the car when she opened the front door again and called Moll, slipping a lead off the hook.

It took five minutes to get to the motorway and forty minutes to reach the airport. The airport's new streaming system meant there were huge signs announcing that you could only wait for five minutes, and had to pay for the privilege. She decided to drive round to the new taxi pick-up on the edge of the main route out. Viv's adrenalin was pumping, so she abandoned the car and ran inside the terminal in the hope that she'd find Sal at the luggage carousel.

She scouted around, read news of the Heathrow flight, and found where the baggage was coming in. Sal wasn't tall and would be swamped by people elbowing to get their cases, but she spotted her going at a pace towards the exit pulling a case like a black armadillo behind her. Viv waved and grinned, but Sal's shocked look wasn't the picture of happiness she'd hoped for. Nonetheless Viv bounced forward and saw Sal soften slightly. They kissed, a chaste effort, and Viv stretched to take hold of the handle of the armadillo. Sal resisted but quickly allowed it.

'Follow me.' Viv marched them back through the taxi rank shelter, full of people waiting with tickets, to her car, which was on a double yellow line with a guy in uniform next to it speaking into a microphone on his head-set.

He glared at them as they approached. Viv pressed the fob and the lights flashed. She opened the boot and swung the case inside, then gestured to Sal to hop in. Sal threw her handbag in beside the case and jumped into the passenger seat, making a fuss of Molly, who bounced all over her. Within seconds Viv had them on the road to Edinburgh, with a quick look in her rear-view mirror to see the irate officer take a photograph of the retreating number-plate.

'So what's with the visit to Fettes?'

Sal was distracted by Moll. 'I said. I had some dodgy communication and I'd like them to check it.'

'Sure, I got that. But why not let me have a look? I'm the one they'll come to if they have any problems.'

Sal didn't respond and continued to fuss over Moll, who was finding it difficult to contain her enthusiasm. They hit traffic at the Gogar roundabout and halted. The silence became difficult to sustain.

'Okay, Sal, what's going on? I've been trying to ring you and it's always gone to answering service or no signal. Did you have it switched off?'

Sal still didn't reply. She sniffed and rummaged around in the glove compartment, grabbed a tissue, but didn't answer, just looked straight ahead.

Viv blew out a huge breath. 'What the fuck is going on?'

When Sal remained silent, Viv, about to explode, suddenly sensed that there must be an answer in her not answering, so she thought through the possibilities. There was no way Sal would behave like this without good cause. What could this mean? Once Viv had reminded herself to be rational she calmed, and thought straight. Eventually it struck her that the correspondence sent to Sal must relate to her, Viv, in some way, and because Sal was employed by Police Scotland she had an obligation to take it to them first.

As they pulled into Fettes car park, Sal spoke. 'So you got there in the end?'

Viv, peeved, nodded with reluctance. 'I still think if you trusted me you'd have let me see it first.'

Sal looked pissed off by this but hurried round to the boot, grabbed her kit, and strode off to the building. Viv wasn't sure whether to follow or wait in the car, until she spotted Sal wedging the door with her boot as she spoke to the duty sergeant over her shoulder.

Viv skipped up the steps and took hold of the door. This was good. Both Viv and Sal had the same clearance at Fettes; not the highest, but high enough to get into the basement and through the first two sets of doors. Sal had warned the techie guys that she was coming in with whatever cloak and dagger issue she had, but they'd be surprised to see Viv, who was strong competition for them in their role as cyber analysts, the polite name for ethical hackers. Viv had been here a couple of months back working a case for Mac. One of her hair clients, a surgeon, had been discovered dirty dealing in organs and she'd been tasked with acquiring incriminating material to corroborate their suspicions. Viv succeeded in getting hold of the info, but not before she'd taken a serious kick in the kidney.

She trotted to keep up with Sal, whose pace didn't reflect a woman who should be suffering from jetlag.

Chapter Twelve

Sal laid her ID card against a small digital panel and the door of the bunker slid open. Viv thought of the miles of corridors running beneath the Edinburgh Accies' playing fields and could only guess at what they were used for. This was the DFU, or Digital Forensic Unit. The whole underground building had been designed during the Cold War. Scotland was peppered with redundant secret bunkers. This one was big enough to hole up lots of dignitaries for long periods of time. They had another door to release before stepping through into a buzzing, blue-grey technical haven. Monitors ran from wall to wall, each screen with a body, equally blue-grey for the want of sunlight, staring at it. Mostly pale, stale males, but also a couple of females who'd obviously picked short straws, otherwise they'd have been bagging Munros or windsurfing on this early spring bank holiday weekend.

Sal headed straight to one particular bloke, who looked up and smiled until he spotted Viv. 'You . . .' He quickly clicked his mouse and his screen went blank. Viv smiled, guessing if he clicked it again all that they'd see was a game of solitaire.

Sal didn't give him time to continue. 'I had to do it by the book, that's why. I know she could do it . . .' She hesitated. 'But that's not the point.' She handed him her laptop. He booted it up and synchronized it with his own console − easier to read detail on his large screen.

Viv now knew that whatever had been sent to Sal, she'd thought it worthy of prosecution. There could be no other reason for doing the analysis in-house. Sal would want a clean history, meaning she'd not want Viv to tinker around leaving any kind of unusual cyber trail. Not that she would, but people who weren't techie always believed what they saw on the TV. There are ways of cleaning up as you go with a computer, which only another hacker with a certain understanding would know. Viv belonged to a group called 'Hacker Crackers', but the fewer people who knew about that the better.

'Bingo!' The bloke looking at the laptop smiled up at Sal. 'Not a professional job, thank goodness.' He beckoned to Sal who looked over his shoulder. Viv stepped closer to view the screen and could see what he meant. On a largely black screen there was a list of numbers and symbols, among those lay the key to the servers through which the transaction had had to pass before it reached Sal's inbox. On seeing that it was an easy process, Viv wandered across to a seat and rolled it over to the guy's left. Everyone had their own way of tracing information but there were short routes and long routes. She favoured the former but was keen to see what kind of meal he'd make of it.

'Sal, you do realize that this can't take us to the person who struck the keys. Only to the account. This is only the beginning.'

Sal nodded to Viv. 'They've really got it in for you, Viv, and whoever they are they know far too much about both of us.'

Viv screwed up her eyes. 'What exactly did the email say?'

'Once we're through here I'll show it to you. But the person was light on grammar. Not a comma or full stop to be had.'

'So the question is, are they young and don't do punctuation? Or trying to make us think that they can't use it? Who, or what kind of person would do that? Let's say they are young. It would be their norm to write without punctuating but they'd more likely use text speak.'

'No, it wasn't like that. But I'll show you when Gordon's through.' Sal's irritation was barely disguised.

Gordon didn't look up from his task, rapidly tapping on keys and staring at the screen.

Viv was getting tetchy and tried to take a deep breath without being noticed. Sal gave her a severe eyeballing. Viv glanced round the room, intrigued by the other analysts with their heads down, and thought that if she had to do what they were doing all day she'd go mad. For her it was the joy of breaking a system whose designer believed it impenetrable that gave her a kick, but, like having a vindaloo, if she had to have one every night it would soon lose its appeal.

'Bingo!' Gordon exclaimed again.

Viv raised her eyebrows but wasn't too hopeful. He turned and gestured to her to check the screen. He had traced both the server and the system that had sent it. The next tricky job was for him to find the actual machine that had been used. Machines, like most things these days, had a kind of DNA but within a corporate setting their numbers could be so close that it could take an age to find.

Sal said, 'So what now?'

Gordon glanced at Viv then across to Sal. 'Well, there are different ways of getting into a big system, of which this is a part.' He hesitated.

Viv stepped in. 'I think what he means is that there's a quick way which is high risk and a slow way which is less risky but infinitely more dull.'

Gordon nodded. 'And you forgot to mention that both leave a trail that could be traced back to my console at Police Scotland, which they're not going to like unless there's a conviction. So if this is for your personal attention and you're not going for . . .'

Sal interrupted him. 'Oh no. This is war. They've managed to get details about finances and legal advisors . . . they couldn't have got those without illegal means.'

Viv raised her eyebrows again, confused at Sal's vagueness. 'What do you mean, Sal? You think they've hacked into a bank account or solicitors' system or what?'

Sal nodded. 'Yep. I do. All of the above. How else could they have that kind of information? I don't . . .' She hesitated. 'Wait a minute. In the early days when I first started here I used another account. I never use it now and I think I deactivated it.'

'Let's see if we can get that up.' Viv edged closer to Gordon's side and said, 'May I?' then continued, 'It could be someone on the inside, an employee.'

Gordon, only concerned with minding his own back, ignored

Viv and Sal's exchange and said without sincerity, 'No problem. But I'll have to follow every move you make in case I have to justify the access – you're on my login.'

In an attempt at being gracious, Viv rolled her chair back. 'Sorry. On you go. I just thought . . .'

Sal shot her another glare and Viv didn't finish her sentence. This kind of attitude was exactly why she wasn't a permanent member of staff here or anywhere else. Viv was known not to play by team rules unless her arm was twisted up her back, but it was for those very same reasons that Mac and the NTF employed her.

The windowless room was making her feel claustrophobic. The whirr of air-conditioning units and cooling fans on computers maintained a constant hum. A galley type kitchen situated at the far end of the room had floor-to-ceiling glass along one side with no door, and a small sink, a microwave, and a kettle were built in to make sure no one could hide. To the right of this an area for relaxation was laid out with two sofas and a large, square coffee table with newspapers and magazines strewn over it. Liquids and computers were a lethal combination, and it was compulsory to keep drinks away from consoles. Viv glanced round the room and counted three, out of a couple of dozen desks, without cups at them. She smiled, delighted that she wasn't in a room full of arse-lickers, although there was no evidence of Gordon rebelling.

The constant clicking of keys must surely fade into the background. Viv tried to imagine being in the room without anyone else there. She recognised a couple of floor-to-ceiling secure cupboards that Mac had brought her to when he supplied her with a special pack and phone for an NTF job. She couldn't remember returning them. Her own phone rang. Sal looked up but quickly returned her gaze to whatever Gordon had discovered. Viv guessed that Sal's old account may well have been deactivated but that didn't mean the information stored there couldn't be accessed.

Viv checked the caller ID and answered with one finger in her ear. 'Hi, Rosanna, what can I do for you?'

'Oh, Viv, something's come up and I'm desperate to have my hair done. Is there any chance that you could . . .'

'Er, I'm not actually working this week. Could it wait 'til next . . .' Rosanna was known for her dramatic hair days.

'Not really. I could get a blow-dry somewhere else, but it needs cut and I wouldn't let anyone else near it with scissors . . . I could come to you if that helped.'

Viv was thinking on her feet. Where was her hairdressing kit? Could she squeeze in a quick cut while Sal was working with Gordon? She glanced around the room as if the answer was somewhere there. Sal's head was still down with Gordon's, and the info they were after would take as long as it took.

'Look, Rosanna, can I ring you back? Give me ten minutes.'

'Sure. I'm going out in a bit, but leave a message if I'm gone.'

Then, turning to Sal, 'Sal, any thoughts on how long this might take?'

Sal stared at Viv as if she was a naughty child who kept interrupting. 'No idea.' She sighed. 'As long as it takes. Why? You got somewhere to be?'

Viv, pissed off at the irritation in Sal's voice, tried to put it down to jetlag. She nodded and checked her watch. 'Actually, I could have somewhere to go, if this was going to take another hour.'

Sal shrugged and put her arms up in resignation. Viv rubbed Sal's arm but felt her tense and withdraw it. There was more going on here than jetlag but now was not the time to start unpacking it. 'I'll be back within the hour. I'll take the car and Moll, she'll need a bit of exercise before we drive back to Doune.'

Sal blurted out. 'Do you need to come back to Doune?'

Viv was shocked, hurt. 'What? . . . What do you mean, do I need to come back to Doune? All my stuff's there . . . clothes and . . .'

Sal chewed on the inside of her cheek but nodded and turned her attention back to the screen.

Viv, unsure of what to say, headed for the door but couldn't get out because she didn't have her own ID card with her. A guy, whose desk was close to the door, stood and flashed his card in front of the panel and the door released.

'Thanks.'

'No probs.'

Once in the corridor she stopped and scratched her head with both hands. What was going on? Sal wasn't prone to crazy behaviour. Tiredness aside, she wouldn't speak to Viv like that. What would she have to believe to act as if Viv was the enemy?

In no mood now to speak to Rosanna, Viv drove to the other side of Inverleith Park and took Moll for a run. Just within the perimeter of the boundary the council had laid out a military style obstacle course. Viv decided to give it a go. The first challenge she encountered got the better of her. She was too ruffled to concentrate. Two long narrow logs that she had to run over lengthwise required spot-on co-ordination. Viv's inner critic stepped up to the plate and on her second attempt she darted over them without even looking at her feet. The next obstacle, a high bollard, she leapfrogged without hesitation, the only way to do it. By the time she'd completed her first round she felt ready to ring Rosanna but her call went straight to a message service. She could now tackle Sal. Her defences were repositioned.

Viv knew that she could never know another's mind but she could infer a lot from their behaviour. She traced Sal's first sign of annoyance to the phone call where she said she was sick of Stetsons. Something must have happened at the airport, or just before. But what had it to do with Viv? Maybe nothing. Maybe Viv was just the first object around for Sal to target. How much of the email was to do with Viv? And if it was all about Viv, why send it to Sal?

Too many questions. She tried Rosanna again. Viv hated to disappoint a client and on the whole bent over backwards to accommodate their needs but where was she going to be?

Rosanna answered. Viv said, 'Hi, if there was a chance that you could get someone to blow-dry it, to tide you over, I'll be back in

Edinburgh on . . .

She was interrupted. 'Actually, Viv, it's not so desperate. I managed to find my Vent brush. I'd mislaid it and been trying to use an old round thing. Anyway, it's fine. Everything is fine, and I've got something in the diary for two weeks' time. I'm sorry, I shouldn't have hassled you. You know what I'm like if I can't get my hair right.'

Viv did, but Rosanna was not the only client whose life collapsed if their blow-dry didn't work.

With one less thing to think about, she rang Mac. 'Hi, Mac, dinner is off.'

'Oh, okay. How's Sal?'

'Don't ask. I can't work out what's going on with her. Three days ago she was dying to get back to see me and now she can hardly look me in the eye. She's had this email which, I think from the way she's acting, must be frickin' apocalyptic. Hang on, there's another call coming through. I'll have to take it. It's Sal. Speak later' . . . 'Hey, are you done? I'm only five minutes away.'

'I'll wait in reception.'

As she drove into the car park Sal trotted down the steps of the front entrance. Nothing about the building was pleasing. Function over form.

'The email came from someone who works for, or around, NHS Scotland. Gordon traced it to a machine in Edinburgh Royal Infirmary. You know anyone who works there, Viv?'

'A couple of people, but no one that'd do anything to hurt me.

How about you?'

Sal sat silently looking ahead as they drove out on the Queensferry Road. The pious Queen Margaret had taken this route to catch a ferry she had organized for pilgrims to cross the river Forth to St Andrews. It ran for almost a thousand years before the bridges were built. But Viv and Sal were no pilgrims and were heading for the Bo'ness turn-off, before the road bridge, then onto the M9.

'Viv . . . someone got into my financial accounts and my files at the solicitors'.'

Viv snapped, 'Yeah, I got that back there.' This came out more abruptly than she'd intended, so she softened. 'So have you contacted the lawyers yet? There has to be an emergency number for them.'

'They've not only hacked my account.' Sal looked over at Viv who turned briefly and caught her look of concern.

'What? What are you saying . . . or not saying as it seems?'

'They've hacked into yours as well.'

Now Viv was confused. 'How . . . I mean how is that possible? Why would anyone want both of our account details?'

'I'm only going to guess here, but it may be about inheritance.'

Viv took her foot off the accelerator unconsciously, but the driver behind didn't delay in tooting. She gesticulated and put pressure back on the accelerator, digesting what Sal had said. They were used to unpacking what motivated people but at the moment Sal was more qualified to make this judgement since she had all the information.

'But why would you keep this from me? Why wouldn't you let me check that email's path? And how do you know that they've got access to my account?

Sal shook her head. 'Because they quoted from your details as well as mine. So I am assuming that you didn't hand those over and that they've accessed your account and your solicitor's files.'

'Okay.' Viv bit her lip and tried to keep calm. 'What exactly did the email say?'

'I've had three. Mostly bad-mouthing you.'

Viv thumped the steering wheel. 'Shit! This is crazy . . . I can't talk about it until we get home. I need to see exactly what they've sent you.'

The rest of the journey took twenty minutes and neither spoke until they reached the house. When Viv said, 'You don't want me to stay. Fine. But I need to see that email . . . before I head back to Edinburgh.'

The temperature dropped a few degrees, but they entered the cottage together, where Sal, resigned and exhausted, handed Viv her laptop and trudged upstairs with her case.

Viv automatically reached for the electric kettle, still not convinced of how efficient the Aga was, but decided against making anything. The laptop was still on with direct access to Sal's accounts. Her current email account was the one that they'd sent the threatening email to, but first they had hacked into the deactivated one for information. It struck Viv that perhaps there was more than one person involved. But she soon became so wrapped up and appalled by the vitriol of the correspondence that the notion went into the recesses of her mind.

No wonder Sal was alarmed. She was right, the details they had about both of their finances could only have come from solicitors' files. Details about Dawn's legacy to Viv were there in black and white, and ditto Sal's inheritance from her aunt. Viv, astonished at how much Sal had in assets, was just about to become indignant about Sal keeping secrets when she remembered she hadn't spoken to Sal about all that she had tucked away. They'd never discussed the ins and outs of their income or their properties. Why would they? But whoever sent this knew everything that mattered and was accusing Viv of being a gold-digger, only interested in Sal for what she could get. Viv snorted when she read this. Money was so far off Viv's radar that this was clearly from someone who had never met her.

Viv and Sal had on occasion mentioned how grateful they were not to have to worry about where the next meal was coming from but they'd never spoken about details. Viv had no idea that Sal owned the whole estate, tower house, cottages, barns, fishing rights etc. etc. And seeing in print what she owned herself made her squirm in her seat. Her solicitor had set it out for her at the beginning, but she'd more or less buried the information, not knowing what to do with it. What she did remember was telling the solicitor that she didn't want it, and that they'd have to find a way of 'dealing' with it. But in the meantime it would be held in a trust until she decided.

A thought crossed Viv's mind that was so ridiculous that she had to entertain it more than once before enough words formed that she might run them by Sal. She took the stairs two at a time but found Sal curled up on the bed fully clothed with her back to the door. Viv gently pulled the duvet over her, closed the door, and returned to the laptop.

Viv decided there was no harm in searching where Gordon had already been. Only she'd take the quick route. The NHS system was complicated but not difficult for someone with her techie skill and she soon had the details of the machine where the email had come from. It was live and Viv could watch the activity. If Viv took Sal's laptop and drove to Edinburgh Royal there was a chance she could catch the person using it in the act, even though they were not making contact with Sal. Suddenly the familiar ping of an email arriving made Viv sit up. They were trying again. How could she track the user? There had to be a way. Could she get to Edinburgh and back before Sal stirred? Viv knew Sal would be livid if her laptop disappeared. But hey ho. It would be worth it if Viv could catch whoever it was. Before she set out she sent an email from her phone to a friend who knew slightly more than she did about tracking, and by the time she'd been to the loo and was heading out the door she'd received a reply. Her own information was up to date but her chum had attached an app that would help maintain the strength of the signal. So long as she didn't lose the connection on Sal's laptop she'd be able to go to within a few metres of where the culprit was working. Viv forwarded the app to Sal's laptop, making a mental note to remember to remove it before she brought it back, then she was off.

Chapter Thirteen

It was a long shot. The Rav's petrol gauge was showing red, and there was no way she'd make it to a fuel stop on the motorway. She prayed that the village station was still open and punched the air when she saw its lights on. Once the tank was full she felt confident that she could get to Edinburgh and back without Sal knowing she'd been gone. Saturday night before seven o'clock the roads were quiet and Viv belted down the M9 in under an hour. The Royal Infirmary was on the east side of Edinburgh so it meant dual carriageway all the way.

The hospital car park was busy and she had to circle for five minutes before finding a space. She ignored multiple signs asking if she'd purchased her ticket and headed straight in the front door. Once inside she grabbed a chair and made a few entries on Sal's laptop. The battery was low but Viv crossed her fingers in the hope that there was enough back-up to get her to the console, and the originator of this activity. She marched along corridors, took the stairs at a pace, then suddenly the signal disappeared. 'Shit!'

A young man striding by with his ID card flapping on a ribbon round his neck, glanced at her and shook his head, not because of her expletive, but because simultaneously her mobile rang and she'd automatically reached for it, a total no no in the HDU where she found herself. So intent on watching the signal, she hadn't noticed straying into an area of the mechanical sighs and beeps inevitable in intensive care wards. She switched her phone to silent and continued to the nearest corridor. Sal's laptop battery was also on the blink and with gritted teeth Viv marched back down stairs racking her brain for a way to make good this technical hitch. Her first thought was to search for someone in a waiting room with a charger. Even if she got ten minutes plugged in she'd be able to return to the position where she'd lost the signal in the hope that it would kick in again.

Saturday night in A&E meant far too many drunks but it was still worth a try. So, checking the overhead signs, she followed the arrows to the busiest department in the hospital. It was buzzing, but also had many heads bowed, eyes staring at screens, mainly ipads or iphones. No sign of any leads. A nurse came in and shouted a name, which Viv didn't catch because of a wailing child, whose super-sized mother, doing little to comfort it, was tutting and grumbling because no one would give her a seat. Added to this, a group of guys wearing matching green tracksuits were having a caper at the other end of the room, taking riotous selfies. One holding another in a head-lock. Nothing in the world funnier.

Viv about-turned and headed back to the front desk where four receptionists were taking calls and directing people to wards. Eventually one of them had a reprieve and Viv asked, 'Is there a quiet room where . . .?'

The woman pointed to a sign, not interested in Viv finishing her request. 'Try there.' Then she was distracted as her colleague asked her to do something with the computer. 'The Chapel.'

Viv wasn't looking to pray, she was looking for a charger, although at the rate she was going perhaps prayer wasn't such a bad idea. There had to be a charger somewhere. Of all the people that she knew who worked here she couldn't think of one that she'd let in on what she was up to. She wanted to remain anonymous. She leaned against a wall at the bottom of a staircase, the quietest area in the place. She blew out a huge sigh. If she relaxed she'd think straight. Was she on a wild goose chase? The connection was lost, and she hadn't been intelligent enough to grab a charger before she left. Then she remembered a possibility, another real long shot, in the toolbox in her car. She ran back, opened the boot of the Rav and there, among the shiny unused spanners and locking wheel nuts, she found a carton, bought for ninety-nine pence with so many litres of petrol, which contained a selection of connectors that plugged into the lighter socket – but nothing that would do for the Mac. 'Fuck!' was all she could manage as she tossed the carton back into the toolbox.

She looked heavenward at a clearing sky and felt the chilly air begin to seep in beneath her collar. Leaning against the tailgate it dawned on her that she could swap batteries from her laptop to Sal's. She cursed at herself for being such an idiot and set about it. It took longer than she had thought because she couldn't see well enough to negotiate the tiny screwdriver into its back panel beneath the Rav's eco-lighting.

With the live battery in place she booted up Sal's machine

again, but whoever had been online had disconnected. She thumped the passenger seat. 'Damn.' A guy passing pressed a fob to unlock his car, parked opposite Viv, and tossed her an it-can't-be-that-bad glance. She looked the other way before she told him to go to fuck. She climbed into the driver's seat and shut the world out. After a few deep breaths another possibility had her changing the batteries back again. She 'opened' Sal's email account on her own computer and convinced herself that since nobody had died Sal would understand why she'd do this.

Within a few minutes she heard a 'ping'. 'Yes!' The console inside the hospital was back online, which didn't mean that the same person was using it, but what the heck, she ran back into the building and up the stairs, gripping her laptop. A narrow corridor with light wooden doors on either side was where the signal became most insistent. It was in an area for teaching, with seminar rooms and a lecture theatre, both with partial glass doors and no sign of patients. At the end of the corridor Viv passed through double doors. In this area each door was closed, and if the signal was true, behind one of them someone held a grudge against her and Sal. Most doors had a nameplate with a Doctor or Professor prefix. Viv stopped outside the door where the signal blinked consistently, and was intrigued to find Professor S. Sanchez written on the plate. Interesting. Now what? She hadn't really thought this through.

Relieved that the door, although relatively new, had an old fashioned lock, the type that was easy to pick, she stood very still, hoping to hear movement inside. Then the corridor was plunged into darkness. She swore softly, but the second she moved the lights flickered to life again. Her heart raced at the idea of knocking on the door. This connection didn't make sense. If the Steve that Ger was having an affair with was behind the emails, he would be a formidable opponent, both physically – if the need arose – and psychologically. He didn't get a chair in neuroscience by being a dimwit.

Before she'd made a decision, the double doors at the end of the corridor swung open and Viv almost left her skin. A young female doctor, with a luminous pink stethoscope draped on her chest like a fashion accessory, glanced in Viv's direction. But her mind was elsewhere and she stooped to unlock her door, without engaging. Now that she'd come this far, Viv had no choice but to find out what was happening on the other side of the door. Would she confront the person in the room or use an excuse for entering so that she could make an informed judgement? She rapped on the door, didn't wait for an answer, but pushed the handle down and stepped in to find a woman wearing big glasses and a startled look behind a desk with her hands hovering above a keyboard. Another desk in the room also had a computer and a keyboard, but it didn't seem to be awake and the neat pile of papers was a sign that it had been cleared for the weekend.

'I'm looking for Dr Sanchez.'

The woman seemed to relax. 'He's off duty. Can I help?' Her soft, educated accent had a hint of west coast.

Viv replied, 'Probably not. Any idea when he'll be back?'

'Tuesday. Holiday weekend.' She shrugged.

'So he hasn't been in today.'

The woman shook her head. 'Not to my knowledge. I've only been in for the last hour. So I wouldn't swear under oath, but he's supposed to be up north. What was it you wanted to speak to him about?' Her voice was becoming slightly more interrogatory.

Viv smiled her warmest smile. 'Oh, nothing that can't wait 'til Tuesday. But thanks anyway. Bummer that you've had to come in on a bank holiday weekend.'

The woman nodded. 'Not for long, though. Nearly done.'

Viv glanced quickly round the room, checking for any other way in or out, but saw nothing. 'Thanks again.'

She pulled the door closed and, defeated, returned to her car. If the woman was telling the truth and she wasn't staying long, it'd be worth Viv waiting and taking a look around. She checked her mobile but it hadn't been Sal who'd tried to reach her. Viv guessed she was still out for the count. There were lots of exits from the hospital and Viv had to pray that by watching the main entrance she'd catch the woman on her way out. No guarantees.

It was also worth considering what else this could all mean. For a start, would the signal have become even stronger if Viv had gone to the next floor? But for now the fact that the office belonged to Sanchez, a name she'd heard for the first time in the last few days, the woman in his office, whoever she was, was her best shot.

She sat for the next forty minutes and nothing happened. Pissed off, she jumped out of the Rav and walked towards the entrance. It was busier now, with at least two dozen smokers loitering around the main entrance, some even in uniform. Viv had imagined that the whole site was designated non-smoking, not only indoors, but addiction was a strange animal and people went to great lengths to keep habits happy. As she approached the row of cars closest to the building, she spotted, through plate glass windows, the woman marching along the corridor, inside the building. Viv ducked behind a car, then walked in a crouch until she was sure she couldn't be seen.

The woman rummaged in her bag and as soon as she exited the building she paused, lit up a cigarette and edged through the crowd, exhaling the first draw through her nose, an action that, along with being away from her desk and having lost her big spectacles, made her appear more ladette and less officious. Viv marvelled at the sudden change. As if the woman had been playing the part of a PA rather than actually being a PA. Viv stared as the woman distanced herself from the other social pariahs, but continued to draw deeply on her cigarette, before ostentatiously grinding it out beneath the pointed toe of a patent leather stiletto. No notion of popping it in the bin. Viv wasn't in the slightest anti-smoking but she was a take-your-litter-home freak, and it riled her to see someone who should know better, deliberately dump rubbish, however small.

The woman walked straight by where Viv was crouching. She

pointed a fob at the far side of the car park, and the lights of a small dark Toyota flashed. Now Viv had another decision to make. Should she nip back into the building to check the office above, and/or the computer, or should she follow the woman? The woman won and Viv raced back to the Rav.

Creeping out of the car park, Viv kept the Toyota's tail-lights at a safe distance. The woman took a right towards Edinburgh then turned first left onto a narrow road with a row of brick cottages on the right and a high wall running all the way south on the other side. Beyond the cottages, over-hanging mature trees made it feel like driving through a tunnel. An old estate wall on the right had a couple of large solid wooden gates with couch grass growing in front of them, indicating that they hadn't been opened any time lately. At the top of the road, they reached a set of traffic lights and the woman took a dogleg right through an old entrance with large stone pillars topped by carved, moss-covered lions, their giant paws resting on stone globes. No sign of any gates. A casualty of the Second World War?

There was no way that Viv would risk taking the Rav in, so she parked on the main road skipped through the gates and ran down the tree-lined tarmac drive. A vast, Victorian, turreted house loomed out beyond the trees at the end. From the look of the stonework it had recently been restored, and since there were allocated parking slots, it had probably been divided into flats. To the left of the old building stood a block of six incongruous modern flats, each with a parking space; and on the right, another branch of the drive led to what looked like old stables with garages. The Toyota's lights were extinguished in the lane outside one of the wooden-fronted garages and the woman entered a small coach house opposite at the farthest end. Nothing in this area had been part of the restoration. Peeling paint on the door and downpipes was a sure sign that no one was giving the place any TLC.

No sooner had the woman gone in than the porch light came on, and Viv jumped back into the shadow of a rhododendron bush. The woman had kicked off her heels and stood on the step in stockings, lighting another cigarette. Viv, astonished that she'd fill her lungs with nicotine at all, outside in all weathers so that her soft furnishings didn't reek of tobacco, also noted that it had been less than five minutes since her last cigarette. Again the woman had a few draws, releasing the smoke in huge streams through her nose, before flicking the butt into the bushes and returning inside. Within seconds an upstairs light came on and Viv imagined the woman changing out of her office clothes into slouching kit.

Now that Viv knew where to find her there was no point in hanging about, so she made her way back to the Rav, and returned to the hospital, compelled to take a look, even though the office would most likely be locked. She had her ways, though.

The hospital seemed to get busier with less drinking time left on the clock. The later at night the more drunken accidents there were. Feeling confident about where to go and not expecting anyone to be around, she was surprised to spot the female doctor that she'd seen earlier, now locking her own office door.

Viv hesitated, and feigned searching for something in her pockets until the woman disappeared through the double doors. As quickly as she could manage Viv pulled on a pair of surgical gloves and tried the handle, but the door was locked. She pulled out the first of her picks but it failed. She went through six or seven before she heard a reassuring click, amazed, but delighted, that this relatively new hospital hadn't put in a card system – even Fettes were about to upgrade their secure areas from cards to iris recognition. She stepped into the darkness and immediately her foot touched something that didn't feel good. She shuffled back toward the door, feeling that she wasn't alone. She stretched along the wall in search of the light switch. Unlike in the movies, she wasn't about to continue to stumble around in the dark, but she wasn't ready for what she saw.

The bulk of Steve Sanchez lay, face down, spread-eagled on the floor. Not moving and not breathing. 'Shit!' She glanced around just to make sure there definitely wasn't another door in or out, stepped up to the body, and put two fingers on his carotid artery. Nothing. She bumped against the desk and the computer monitor leapt into life, the screen saver a photograph of a stunning looking woman with an arm around two very pretty young girls, all peas in a pod. So, not exactly in love with Geraldine, then? She checked the tidy desk. All the drawers were locked and the papers lying on the top were academic notes and medical journals. The bins were empty. A sweet smell, like mock lavender, rose up from the fabric of the swivel seat and within seconds she was smothering the sound of a sneeze into her upper sleeve. Time to make her exit.

Wondering how long it might be before he was found, officially, Viv steadied her breathing and stepped out of his office. The corridor lights sprang to life. All quiet. She walked back toward the car park, brazenly stopping at the kiosk in the entrance to buy a bottle of water. The journey back to Doune would take less than an hour, but she was parched. The roads were deserted, the sky clear as a bell, but death was death even if she hadn't known him. Could his death have been natural? She wondered about the secretary, if that was in fact who the female had been. The look on his face wasn't contorted; he could have been asleep. There was just enough time to check for signs of a struggle. Nothing, a sign in itself. As she well understood, absence wasn't nothing, it was the space where something should be.

Chapter Fourteen

As Viv turned in through the gates leading to Sal's cottage she heaved a sigh, psyching herself up for the conversation that lay ahead. The cottage was in darkness. Molly barked when Viv stepped up to the porch. She gave the door a light tap but entered without waiting for a reply.

Once Viv had greeted Moll, she spotted Sal. Leaning against the doorjamb in her pyjamas, she spoke quietly, exhausted, 'So where have you been? And dare I ask what you were up to with my laptop?'

Light from the muted TV flickered in the sitting room. Sal gestured for them to go through. She clicked on a couple of lamps and sank onto the sofa. She tapped the space beside her and waited for Viv to join her. Viv was taken off guard and the familiar floral smell of Sal's moisturiser lulled her for a moment. Viv peeled off her jacket and swung it over the back of a chair then took a seat. Rigid, she explained what she'd been up to. Starting with tracking the machine, through to following the secretary home, and finally what she had discovered on breaking into Sanchez' office.

Sal was speechless. Viv was a woman who got results, often by unorthodox means, but results nonetheless. Viv watched as all manner of emotions rolled across Sal's face, until eventually some understanding broke that they were in this together. Her hand edged along the back of the sofa and reached out to Viv's head. 'So what's next?'

Viv tensed and sat forward. She'd come back to Doune to return Sal's laptop but largely to pick up her kit. Sal surely didn't expect her to ignore the attitude that had greeted her earlier?

Viv stood up and rubbed her face. 'D'you mind if I freshen up before I head home?'

Sal looked crestfallen. 'You don't have to go. I'm sorry . . . I was freaked out by what that email said.'

Viv shook her head, an imperceptible shake but enough. She took the stairs to the bathroom, asking herself what would need to happen inside her brain before it would be okay to stay. But the leap was too great after the day she'd had. She needed time to think and she'd do that best at home in her cosy little garret.

Viv wasn't an unpacker, so she didn't take long to get her stuff assembled and carry it down to the hallway. Molly started spinning round in circles as if she too was desperate to get out. Viv crouched and soothed her by stroking her ears. Once her bags were in the car she stared at the front door, knowing she should go back inside and say goodbye. She didn't. She reversed the car into the turning spot and slowly drove down the track. As she reached the estate gates Mac's 4x4 was coming in and blocked her exit. 'Shit!'

He jumped out and came to her window. 'Where are you off to now? I've been trying your mobile for hours.' He grinned, nodding back towards the cottage. 'I imagined you'd be kissing and making up.'

Viv snorted. 'Yeah, well, not quite. What are you doing here?' She checked the clock, imagining it was too late for a social call but it was only nine-fifty. 'I'm heading back to Edinburgh.'

He raised his eyebrows in a question.

She was not prepared to answer. 'Don't ask. I'm knackered – a lot's happened since I saw you last. I can't face it now but I'll give you a buzz in the morning. In fact if you're going in,' she gestured back over her shoulder with her head, 'Sal will update you.'

'I hoped to catch you earlier. Those bones up on Sheriffmuir are mostly for the archaeologists, except for one. Which, as you know, is enough to open a suspicious death enquiry.' He smiled. 'But thankfully not for me. Central will handle it . . . And I drove back over to the hotel. Couldn't find anything that would give us a clue about who broke the window, but wasn't welcomed with open arms by anyone in the bar, so something's going on. I'm wondering if we really did just get caught in the crossfire. Anyway I'd better let you go.' He sighed, with both hands leaning on the roof of the Rav, then tentatively said. 'Everything okay?'

Viv grinned back at him. 'I said don't ask. But since you have No, it's not okay.' She rubbed her eyes. 'However, we've probably traced the person who sent those emails. Come on, Mac, let me past. I'm dying to get home, have a hot bath and sleep like the dead.'

He shook his head. 'I guess there's no point in offering you a bed at mine? I've got a . . .'

She shook her head. 'Sweet of you to offer but I'd rather ge back.' Mac had rescued Viv on more than one occasion and whatever her suspicions he was always honourable.

He sauntered back to the Audi and reversed out of the entrance to let Viv through. She waved and drove slowly along the lane, over Wade's bridge, and onto the main road. Fifty minutes and she'd be climbing the stairs in the West Bow.

The journey took a little over the time she'd estimated, and the whole way her head was full of self-recrimination. Sal was a reasonable woman not in the habit of making rash judgements, so she must have been convinced that Viv hadn't been straight with her. Which meant evidence. She wouldn't have blamed Viv without being convinced by the evidence. So what! What more evidence did she need than Viv's integrity? Sal knew her well enough to believe that she was trustworthy. By the time she'd reached the West Bow, Viv had decided that cooling time was more than necessary. She'd let Sal work out who was worth investing in, Viv, or a complete stranger with dirty info. Then by the time she'd climbed to the top of her stairs, she couldn't have given a rat's arse, and didn't want to hear from Sal or anyone else who doubted her in any way.

On the way upstairs Viv passed a woman standing in the doorway to her flat on the first floor. She'd had very little to do with her beyond a 'good morning'. The woman was a long-standing resident of the building, whereas Viv was relatively new. Her name was Shirley Reid and anything that Viv knew of her she'd heard from Ronnie, her immediate neighbour, also a long-termer and fount of knowledge about all things in the building. Shirley always smelled of healing herbs, and wore dangling earrings, brightly-coloured floaty skirts and baggy tee-shirts. Viv imagined the odd séance being held in the first floor flat, since at least once a month a similarly attired group of people turned up and left a couple of hours later. Although polite to each other neither had made any effort to become better acquainted. So Viv was surprised when, as she went to walk by her today, the woman turned to look her unnervingly in the eye.

Slowly and quietly the woman said, 'Hello. How are you?' Never taking her small, green eyes off Viv's.

Viv, taken aback, stopped with her foot poised over the next step. She turned more fully to face the woman and nodded. 'Er, I'm fine, thanks.' And knowing she couldn't cope with anyone telling them how they actually were, she resisted returning the question. Just as she was about to continue up the stairs, the woman cleared her throat intent on continuing. Viv wondered if she might be after gossip, but the woman said, 'You're not about to go on holiday are you?'

This was weird. Viv stared at the woman's unruly blond hair and said, 'Sadly, not.'

Shirley hesitated, about to speak again, but looked at her feet as if making a decision. 'It's just that I think you might be in danger.'

Viv raised her eyebrows. Too late was the loud reply. 'And what makes you say that?'

Shirley flushed. 'Oh, never mind. I just had a feeling, that's all.

A strong feeling. So I thought I'd let you know. We're not supposed to make predictions but I think if you've seen something that might help someone . . . in danger . . .' She shrugged.

Viv raised her eyebrows in disbelief. This was all she needed, a loony psychic. 'Well, thanks for the warning. I'll bear it in mind.'

'Truly, I've never done this to anyone before. Avoid the coast. The sea was the strongest impression.'

Viv nodded again and moved upstairs. She muttered, 'Thanks again,' over her shoulder. But by the time she reached her own landing she was shaking her head and her eyes were reaching into her hairline. 'What the hell's next?' She whispered to herself as she pushed open the door.

Chapter Fifteen

Viv was woken, in the middle of the night, by the sound of her own sobs. She laid a hand on her chest to ease the weight of melancholy. Breathing deeply she tried to calm the irregular pounding of her heart. She struggled to retrieve snippets of the dream. Something about her and Dawn, her now deceased ex. They'd been out for an evening, everything was unusually pleasant, and Viv's guard was down. Dawn had talked enthusiastically, encouragingly, about their future together. Viv, eager to hear it, felt full of hope until they entered the back garden of their home. It was a warm night and the moon shimmered across a twenty-five-metre swimming pool. The house, like an African safari lodge, was built of wood, on two storeys with a balcony on stilts. A rickety wooden ladder reached up onto the veranda, and light spilled out from every room. At the far edge of the pool an athletic young woman, wearing an orange and navy Speedo swimsuit, sat rocking, bracing her knees. When Viv and Dawn approached, the girl, her face streaked with tears, shouted at Dawn that she'd been waiting for two hours. The depth of Dawn's sympathetic reaction made Viv realise that all the previous talk of the evening had been just that, talk. Distraught, Viv took off running and running, but heavy legs made a rapid escape impossible.

All through the dream Viv's emotions were tested and her heart pounded; and now the weight in her chest felt as if it would crush her. She lay in the dark with the reassuring sound of the odd car driving down Candlemaker Row, their headlights searching her bedroom wall. Viv kept her palm resting on her chest. Slowly her breathing regulated as she unpacked the narrative of the dream. In dreams, however bizarre the story was, there was always a beginning, a middle and an end. Viv was stunned at people who dismissed their dreams as garbage. The brain functioned twenty-four seven; thoughts that came in the form of dreams were as important as any other. Viv paid attention to whatever her mind kicked up, regardless of the time of day.

Slowly, she began to reason with the drama. For starters she and Dawn had never lived together, but perhaps unconsciously she'd hankered after that. It had never been an option. Dawn was incapable of fidelity, endlessly claiming she was married to her work. True, when work involved the new younger members of the orchestra. Unbeknown to Viv, during the last six months of their turbulent relationship, Dawn had been seeing two girls from Edinburgh and one in Inverness. Although at some level Viv had suspected as much, love was cockeyed, and not wanting to believe it she ignored the signs. In the end Dawn's crazy, erratic behaviour wore Viv down. Phone calls in the middle of the night from Dawn, weeping and regretful, confessing her undying love, until the next time she didn't show up for a date. Viv was no doormat and with each call, her commitment was eroded, but there was something about Dawn that kept her wanting, and it was more than between the sheets chemistry.

She heaved a breath. As for the pool, who didn't dream of having a swimming pool? Jungians were always banging on about water as the universal symbol of the unconscious. But whatever Jungians thought, every time she used public baths she had to suspend her beliefs and disbeliefs about what was lurking in the toxic brew.

A further snippet of dream emerged. An unlikely version of her mother entertaining a church committee, since in real life 'Holy Marys' as her mum called church goers, were not part of her mum's life. She'd always criticised them for only doing good works for their own gain and wouldn't have them in the house.

'Go frickin' figure, girl,' was as much as her brain could manage at this time of the night. She jotted the details down, with the intention of giving them her full attention in the morning. She shivered, bundled herself in the duvet, and counted hundreds of sheep off the abattoir lorry and back onto the hill, eventually falling into a fitful sleep.

On waking the next morning Viv felt as if she'd had a kicking. Aching, she rolled over, drew the duvet over her head, and closed her eyes. Worth a try. She wasn't the type to languish in bed. She groaned and reached for the switch on the radio. They were running a piece on the death of a man 'alleged to be one of Edinburgh's most eminent neurologists'. She sat up and stared at the radio, tweaking the volume when her head could no longer stand the high pitch of the female reporter's voice, who screeched into her microphone in an attempt to transcend the traffic noise of a busy hospital car park. The reporter claimed that the professor had died of a heart attack while at work on Saturday night.

'Someone is yanking your chain, girl,' Viv whispered to the radio.

Recalling his screen saver, Viv wondered how Sanchez' wife and children would react to this news, and questioned what Geraldine had told her about their divorce. Ger would be devastated to hear this announcement . . . or would she? Viv groped around her bedside table in search of her mobile. She scrolled through her contacts, determined that she had Ger's number, but no, only an email address. She sent her a quick message but within a few minutes an out of office reply bounced back.

Swaddled in the duvet, she padded through to the kitchen, flipped the kettle on, either for tea or a hot water bottle, she couldn't decide. Every movement took an effort and the person that looked back at her from the bathroom mirror was unrecognisable. Dark rings framed dull eyes, and her skin, usually translucent, looked a khaki shade of grey, and worse still, her tongue felt like a seventies shag pile rug.

Hot water bottle in hand she flopped into bed and was lulled back into a superficial reverie by the low tone of the radio. Eventually her mobile phone vibrated and brought her back to life. It was Sal's number. In no mood to have a deep and meaningful, she let her answering service pick it up.

A tinge of regret tickled at her conscience, but not for long. She cuddled the remaining warmth of the hot water bottle and for the next hour or so indulged in drifting in and out of feeling sorry for herself.

Her phone vibrated again. This time it was Mac. She held her nose and answered with, 'Hi, leave a message. I'm feeling lousy . . .'

'What's up? You think you've overdone being a country girl? I take it you've heard about Sanchez?' Mac might be her friend but he was first and foremost a cop.

Sal must have given him all the details about what she'd done yesterday and this was his none-too-subtle way of checking her out.

'Mind if I drop by for a cup of coffee?'

She groaned. 'No, I really am unwell. I've got a raging head and my muscles . . .'

'I'll take the risk, if it's okay with you? And since you're not going anywhere anytime soon I'll leave it until after lunch. That'll give you time to get a shower and your story straight.'

She stuttered at the last comment. 'What d'you mean . . . get my story straight? Sal gave you a straight version.'

'What? Sure. Straight as a nine bob note. I didn't come up the Clyde, Viv. See you about half one.'

He rang off and she threw her phone onto a chair laden with clothes that needed sorting. 'Shit! Shit! Shit!' Viv had gone to

Sal's for some R&R. She should have holed up and not been tempted to go running round the moors or out with soaking wet hair to pursue a long shot. Or for that matter bolting off to Edinburgh in search of that signal. The clock read twelve ten. She decided that if she was going to be of any use to herself or Mac, she'd better pop a few pills.

The cupboard in the bathroom offered an out-of-date box of Paracetamol, two of which she downed with bottled water that had long lost its fizz. She gagged as one of the pills lodged in her throat, but continued towards the shower in anticipation of a modern day miracle.

As ever, she felt a whole lot better with clean hair and exfoliated skin. She slipped into some jogging pants, an over-sized flannelette shirt, and her favourite bed-socks, knitted, as a Christmas gift, by a uni friend. One of the best presents she'd ever had. Three-ply, homemade bed socks, what's not to like about a friend who does that? She checked her emails and listened to a message of apology from Sal on her phone. She answered messages from hair clients. No emotional turmoil required for that.

When the buzzer went she blew out a sigh but wandered to the speaker, and was just about to release the door when a voice, not Mac's as she'd expected, said, 'Doctor Fraser?'

'Who's asking?'

'You don't know me, but I was wondering if we might have a chat?' The voice was male and cultured.

Flustered, Viv hesitated before deciding. 'Er, no, this isn't a good time. What's it about anyway?'

'I'd rather not say . . . '

Abruptly Mac's familiar voice interrupted. 'Hey, Viv, you going to let me in?'

Then there was a scuffle and Mac shouted, 'Back in a minute.'

Viv stood listening for any sign of action but hearing nothing save traffic on the cobbles outside she left the door and went to put the kettle on. It took a few minutes before Mac returned and she buzzed him in.

'What the hell was that about?' Seeing Mac back in an immaculate suit and crisp white shirt caused her insides to flutter. She laid her hand across her front, reminding herself not to go there.

He grinned. 'Oh, nice to see you too . . . you at the end of the queue for social graces or what?'

'Fuck off, I'm not in the mood.'

'I gather that. I followed the guy who was speaking to you. There was something weird about the way he was hogging the entry phone, and when I leaned over him he shoved his elbow into my sore rib . . . well anyway he backed off at speed, and jumped into a black Toyota with a female driver waiting for him outside Bella's. I've got the registration number.' He handed Viv his phone. 'Recognise this?'

Viv nodded. 'The other night when I was tracking that email account, the one that Sal . . .'

'Yeah, yeah, I know the one you're talking about.' He gestured with his hands for her to keep her story rolling.

'Well, I found a secretary or PA in Sanchez' office and I followed her. She got into a Toyota, but it was dark and I couldn't see the exact colour. Coincidence?' She went through to the bedroom to fetch her mobile. 'Here. I took a note of the number.' She compared their screens. 'Yep, same car.'

'I'll have it checked.' He pressed a quick dial and read his PA the number before turning back to Viv. 'So you want to run through what you did yesterday?'

She glared at him. 'No. I've got nothing to say that Sal won't have told you.'

'How about you humour me? Let's pretend that you didn't tell Sal absolutely everything.'

Like a recalcitrant child she sighed ostentatiously. 'I went in search of the signal from the computer that had sent the emails to Sal. It wasn't difficult.'

He raised his eyebrows.

She ignored him and continued. 'I traced it to Edinburgh Royal Infirmary and when Sal zonked out I thought I might as well take a look.'

He raised his eyebrows again. 'And you did this how?'

She eyeballed him. 'You really want to know?'

He nodded. 'Indeed I do.'

'Well there's a way to set . . .' She sighed, knowing how dull the explanation would sound. 'You know when you use Facebook and there are a list of names that are active on the side?'

His eyes widened. 'Yes, I do. But with Facebook we're still in legal range.'

'Oh, for fuck sake, you don't really want to know then. Let's just say I found a way to follow the signal.'

'Illegally, all the way to Edinburgh?'

Choosing to ignore the bit about whether it was legal or not, she replied, 'God, Mac, it's a fifty minute drive not the dark side of the fucking . . . oh anyway. When I got there I lost the signal for a bit. Then Sal's battery ran out and I had to do a bit of fiddling around before I found the signal again. Naturally I went to investigate, and found a woman inside the office which had Sanchez' name on the door.'

'And you know Sanchez how?'

'Well, I don't. I only saw him for the first time the other day. A friend of mine is having a relationship with him and . . . well never mind that.'

'No, no, go on. Fill me in. That's exactly the kind of stuff that you didn't tell Sal or . . .'

She glared. 'I bumped into my friend from university days, Geraldine, in the café in Doune. She was upset and was going to come back to the cottage and have a chat but when we went outside she spotted her man, the very one that she was upset about. Some guy . . . a professor of neurology. I'm sure she said Stephanos Sanchez – a huge brute of a guy. Anyway she, Ger, went off with him. End of.' She shrugged. 'I could have passed him for all I know: some of the corridors at the hospital were packed. It makes sense that he was there now, though.'

Mac rolled his hand again for her to continue. 'I'm still listening, and by the way, when exactly did you bump into her? Was it before you were attacked or what?'

VIv thought for a moment. 'Actually I saw her before. What? . . . you seeing a connection?'

He nodded. 'Could be. But carry on.'

She heaved another sigh and glanced heavenward. He smiled and gestured again for her to keep going.

Peevishly she continued. 'As I've said, I followed his PA from the hospital car park to where I think she lives, which luckily wasn't far. Then I returned to the hospital. To take a quick peek.'

Mac shook his head. 'No notion of abiding by the law, I suppose?'

She frowned at him. 'Why would I start now? Anyway, as I was saying, it wasn't difficult to get into his office and there, lying face down on the floor, was a huge body. I immediately retreated and drove back to Sal's, but things weren't so good there and as I left, I bumped into you on the drive home. Voila! That's the whole truth and nothing like the truth.' She crossed her heart.

'Freudian slip, though. Nothing but the truth is what you should have said.'

She was about to deny that she'd said it incorrectly but didn't think it was worth the hassle. 'What-fucking-ever!'

'I think we'll eliminate your prints from the office. So, what did you touch?'

She feigned shock. 'Me, touch anything?'

'Yes, you.'

'I had frickin' gloves on. So there won't be any prints.'

'What, you had gloves on when you saw the secretary?'

'No, but I only opened the door and stuck my head in.' Then as a second thought she added, 'My boot prints will be there, though.' SOCOs wouldn't miss a trick they were bound to get a partial of one, or both of her boots. Again she'd be eliminated from the enquiry so long as she was above board about that.

'I rest my case. Your prints are in the system so we can call those up and count you out . . .' He stared at her questioningly.

'Of course you can . . .'

He nodded. 'Okay. But you know the risk I'm taking if I do?'

She stifled a yawn. 'Yes, I do. Thank you.'

'I'm serious, Viv. If they find any sign of you in that office . . . even a single hair.'

With mock assurance she replied, 'They won't. I promise they won't.'

'Still, you'd better get your boots and I'll photograph the soles.'

Viv stepped out to the hall and returned with her boots. He took photographs with his iphone. Then her landline rang. Her eyes widened as she listened to the caller. A shrill voice made its way into the room. 'Mand, slow down. Tell me where you are and I'll come . . .' She was cut off in her stride as her sister, Amanda, screeched into her ear. 'Okay. Cameron Toll. I'll be ten, fifteen minutes tops.'

Before Mac could say anything she was pulling on her boots, grabbing her bag and jacket at the same time.

Chapter Sixteen

She raced out leaving Mac at her front door. She leapt downstairs four at a time, missing the worn step. By the time she reached Manda in the car park of the shopping centre, she was surrounded by strangers trying to help. Manda was hysterical.

A woman said, 'I've called an ambulance.'

Mand spotted Viv and shooed the others away. Her waters had broken and the driving-seat of her brand new Lexus looked beyond recovery. Viv managed to edge Mand out of the car and tentatively guide her into the Rav. Mand, trying to remember how to breathe, had very few words, other than expletives, to say to her sister.

Viv drove like a maniac to the hospital with Manda screaming and breathing loudly in equal measure. Viv knew there was no point in trying to comfort or reason with Mand, whose temper, even on a calm day, was never worth competing with. Viv took control by being practical. On arriving she shouted for a porter to bring a wheelchair and elbowed the smokers out of the way. Once they were on their way down the correct corridor Viv thought about her car being clamped. 'I'll be back in a minute.'

'No!' Mand screamed. 'No! . . . Please don't leave me. Please, Viv, don't . . . I'm terrified.' With tears streaming down her face, her pleading touched something primal in Viv, and she took hold of her sister's hand and closed her eyes at the pain of Mand's returning squeeze.

There was no question of rescuing the car. They were swept up by an adept porter, who'd clearly done this many times before. As they reached the maternity unit everything began to move into slow motion for Viv. Manda's screams were replaced by a horrible whimpering noise that Viv could hardly believe was human, far less her immaculate and controlled sister. Viv's hand was still being crushed but there was nothing she could do. At one point it occurred to her to ask where her brother-in-law was, but when she opened her mouth it was as if Mand anticipated what she was going to say and shook her head so violently that Viv just said, 'It's okay. It's okay.'

A midwife approached and pointed to a cubicle, and the porter, who Viv imagined was grateful that English was not his first language, pushed Mand through, then, along with a nurse, helped her onto a trolley-bed. Viv's own aches receded in the drama, although she distractedly massaged the hand that Manda had squashed, relieved that the professionals had taken over. There was no mention of the hypno-birth plan that Mand had talked incessantly about. Even Viv's mum seemed able to remember exactly how Manda's birth would go. Mand looked and sounded pitiable.

Viv could hear her mother's voice saying, 'She'll no have her worries to seek now.' Which was exactly how Viv felt. She and her sister had a chequered adult history. Their childhoods were far enough apart for competition not to be a problem. Viv had always looked up to, and admired Mand, who was the beautiful one, the one with the brains, always stylish, a head turner. Viv, athletic in body and mind, wasn't worried about getting muddy. It really hadn't been until Manda met her husband, a corporate whizz, who travelled the globe leaving Mand, adorned in Escada, to take care of their clinical white house, that things deteriorated between them, as if Viv and her mum weren't good enough for her new company wife image. Seeing her sis in this state suddenly dissolved their differences and reminded Viv of how much they had in common; how the family bond really did matter.

When the midwife came out from behind the curtain she beckoned Viv over. 'It won't be long. Is there a father?'

'Yes there is, but I've no idea where he is.'

The midwife shrugged as if nothing would surprise her. 'I take it you'll be at the birth then?'

Viv was horrified by that idea, but her choices were limited and she thought she could probably manage it. She nodded. 'Okay. I expect if she wants me there . . .'

Mand, clearly listening between puffs from behind the curtain, screeched, 'Of course you'll be there.'

Viv drew the curtain back, and shocked at how pathetic Mand looked, felt a lump rising in her throat. She swallowed hard, suddenly reflecting that she was unlikely otherwise to see a birth in her life, and that really it was a privilege to be asked.

Manda sobbed. 'Vivi, you mustn't leave me.'

Hearing her childhood name brought Viv closer to the trolley.

How strange that Mand needed her now. At least a decade had passed since Mand and Viv had been on generous terms. Communication between them, when they had managed to speak at all, was more thistle and bristle than thoughtful. But old conflicts appeared to vaporise now.

The bustling and chatter around the bed seemed part of another world until the nurse bellowed, 'We're on the move!'

It was code for something, because the trolley was whirled round and pushed through double doors leading to another corridor. Viv felt Mand's grip release and watched as her eyelids fluttered. Was she passing out?

'What's going on? What's happening? Where are you taking her?' Viv's cool was no longer feasible.

'Surgery!' someone yelled. And Viv was man-handled out of the way.

She watched as Mand was rolled through another set of doors out of sight. Viv leant against a stainless steel wall, sweat trickling down her forehead as she rummaged in her pocket for a tissue. Aware of her heart racing, she waited. And waited. Eventually the nurse returned, and was about to walk straight past. Viv caught her arm.

'Where is she and what's happening?'

'The baby's turned.'

'What does that mean?'

The nurse looked directly into Viv's eyes as if assessing her strength, 'Breech with complications.'

Viv knew enough to realise this wasn't good news. 'What happens now?'

'Not sure. It's too late to turn the baby back. They might cut her, try with forceps, more likely perform a section, though.' Suddenly she softened. 'She's in the best hands. I'd go and get a coffee or something. She'll be at least an hour.'

Viv trailed behind the woman, who was almost as wide as she was tall. She wondered if she should ring her brother-in-law. Mand's reaction to her earlier comment didn't instil confidence that his arrival would be welcomed. But it was his child too. She made for the exit and joined the posse of smokers before she remembered she'd abandoned the Rav. It was nowhere to be seen and her anxiety took a different shape. She loafed back into reception and pointing outside she explained that she'd had to leave her car. The woman assured her that all was well and that it had been towed to the far side of the car park with all the others.

Viv, not convinced of the Rav's safety, went in search and overcome by relief felt herself welling up when she spotted it at the end of a row. A few deep breaths later and she was finding reason again. She scrolled through her phone but couldn't find her brother-in-law's number. A valid excuse for not making contact. Mac had left a message asking if she was okay. She tried his number but it went straight to his messaging service. Another message from Rosa, a client, piqued her interest but she'd have to make do with a text in reply.

The coffee shop was a vast improvement on the Old Royal

where volunteers from the WRI, not that she had anything against them, were only there between ten and four, and served tea that you could stand your spoon up in or instant stuff which couldn't be called coffee. The reassuring chug and squeal of steam reducing milk to a light froth made her spirits rise. Cappuccino accompanied by an oversized lemon muffin would certainly improve her energy level, at least in the short term. She slid into a seat where the table had had a cursory wipe. A quick scan assured her there were no children within spitting distance.

Why had Manda phoned her? It was so left field. Viv munched on the muffin, and tossed ideas around in her mind. Was her brother-in-law still around, or had Mand finally bitten the bullet and dumped him? No way. She dismissed the notion, sure that her mum would never have been able to keep that secret. Although their mum didn't remember everything she'd had for breakfast, she believed that Mand had married above herself, 'an angel' she called him. If there had been a rift, she'd have been so disappointed, there'd be no way she'd have kept it to herself. So, where the hell was he? What kind of husband beetles off round the world, when his wife is nine months pregnant? 'Selfish sod.' Realising that she'd said this out loud she scanned her periphery to check if anyone had noticed. Her cappuccino was at the perfect temperature to gulp down and with that done she headed back to where she'd left Mand.

Slightly worried that something might have gone wrong, but also a little disappointed that she hadn't, after all, been present at her first birth, now she wondered if she'd have stayed upright, or i she'd have embarrassed herself by fainting. She smiled; maybe i had worked out for the best.

She looked for the nurse who'd sent her for coffee but couldn' see her. She tried to speak to another nurse, this one wearing only white whereas the other had had navy trim on her uniform Everyone in trousers and loose fitting tops with pockets these days Must make life easier not having the worry of laddering tights. Fo a moment she recalled a time in childhood when she'd been ir hospital; the swish of starched uniforms and the absurd headgea had done nothing to reassure her that she was in safe hands. She spotted the nurse she was looking for and skipped to catch her before she disappeared again through the double doors into the inner sanctum.

'Is my sister all right?'

The nurse looked quizzically before registering who she was 'Yes.' She hesitated. 'Yes, she's fine.'

Viv, noting her reluctance, continued, 'And the baby?'

The nurse nodded and pointed to a sign. 'Follow those signs and they'll take you to a ward. Ask at the desk and they'll point you ir the right direction.'

Viv felt she had been got out of the way. Nonetheless she dutifully followed the signs, which led her to the ward where her sister was recovering. Seeing her own reflection in the ward's window against the darkness outside, Viv realised how late it must be. She glanced round in the hope of a clock and found a digital read out on a radio belonging to a woman two beds away from Manda. It was five-forty. My God, what had she been doing all day? That must be wrong. There was no way of checking and she didn't want to pull out her mobile in case she got caught. There were threatening notices everywhere around the hospital and the walls at the desk had been no exception.

Chapter Seventeen

Manda was asleep, or at least completely zonked out, and when Viv whispered to her she didn't stir. It struck Viv that this would be the time to find her brother-in-law, so she retreated to the car park and Googled the number of the company he worked with.

It was a long shot anyone being at their office this late on a Sunday let alone a holiday weekend, but it was all she had. She thought he must be abroad so was surprised when a snippy male receptionist put her straight through. 'Hi, Derek, it's Viv.'

'Amanda's sister Viv?' This pissed her off. Did he know a string of Vivs? He must have recognised her voice but would do anything to wind her up. 'Yes, Mand's sister. She's at the Royal and I assumed you'd like to know.'

With concern in his tone he asked, 'What's the matter? Is it serious?'

What was going on? There was no way he could feign ignorance of the baby. But Viv knew so little of Mand's life that anything could have happened.

'Look, Viv. She probably hasn't mentioned that we've . . .'

'Stop! Don't tell me, you're no longer together?'

'We haven't been together for the last . . . ' And his most sarcastic voice, 'Oh what is it? Seven, eight months?'

Realising why Mand had been so cross when she'd been on the

verge of mentioning him she said, 'Never mind. I shouldn't have called.' She cut the connection, slipped the phone into her pocket and rubbed her hands over her face. He mustn't know about the baby. Mand must have kept it from him. Why? Good reason, Viv assumed.

She'd been shocked when Mand told her she was pregnant, and wondered how their oh so perfect life style would accommodate the messy, dribbly, but perhaps even joyful, life of a child. Mand must have decided she wanted a baby more than the constant worry of dirtying the white carpets. Theirs was a shoes-off-at-the-door household. Was Mand still in the house? She was too quick to cut that call. He'd have spilled the beans or at least laid them out neatly before her. He was a man who took anal retention to dizzying depths, with a weekly manicure and monthly top-up of professional tooth whitening. And although Mand had found his OCD charming in the beginning, Viv had hoped her sister would see the disadvantages of living like a slave. This, a baby, was a major crack in a dam, that wouldn't heal however many fingers were jammed in it. Viv smiled then tried to guess what it must have cost Mand to be on her own for all this time, with morning sickness and the terror of actually giving birth.

Viv wandered back into the ward and sat at the bedside until a nurse came by to check Mand. 'Where's the baby?' Nervous of the reply.

'He's in the special unit . . . Not for long, though.' The nurse must have caught the look of concern that crossed Viv's face and continued, 'No, he's fine. We just wanted Mrs Fraser to get some rest. You can see him from the corridor if you like. Follow me.'

Viv, distracted by the nurse calling Manda Mrs Fraser, trailed behind her out of the main ward and into a side ward. Mand now using her married name? What the heck had been going on? As soon as Mand had married, Viv had backed off. She just didn't get Derek, or any bloke whose skin looked as if he'd bathed in Irn Bru. But why would she? Few men had inspired her since her dad died and Derek, for all his intelligence, was a gonad-rubbing golfer, who couldn't have floated her boat if he'd been Noah. This was not to say she didn't like golf, she did, but not when it was about cosy corporate back-slapping. She shuddered as she recalled the way he behaved towards Mand. Once, in the early days, Viv had been on a rare visit, when Derek had leaned over the back of their ridiculously expensive leather sofa, stretched out his empty glass and said to Mand. 'Refill . . . and don't spill it this time . . . it costs a fortune.'

Viv's blood boiled recalling his arrogance. But Mand had made her choice and now it seemed she'd made another without Viv or their mum knowing her circumstances. Their mum would be devastated at the news of Derek being out of the frame, although the baby would go some way to set that to rights.

The hospital nursery was as she'd seen in movies. Rows of incubators lined up with pink and blue blankets either over the occupants or hanging on the rail at the end of the tiny cots on wheels. The nurse pointed to Amanda's baby.

Viv's eyes widened at the tiny creature with its shock of red hair. 'Oh, my God,' she gasped. 'He's such a wee sweetie!' She sensed that the nurse had heard this kind of utterance a million times before, but she still smiled.

She grinned at Viv. 'I can't let you hold him without the mother's permission but we can wheel him through to her now. She should be awake.' The cot, with tyres designed to scale Ben Nevis, rolled silently back to the bedside. Mand struggled to sit up and Viv tried awkwardly to help but the nurse stepped in and hoisted her efficiently, leaving her propped up on two pillows. The baby stretched its tiny hands and legs and let out the strangest noise.

Mand looked at the nurse, who grinned. 'There'll be a lot more where that came from.' She lifted Viv's brand new nephew into his mother's arms, and Mand, with tears rolling down her cheeks, stifled a sob. The baby, like a marsupial, knew instinctively where to nuzzle for food. Viv, embarrassed, said she'd wait outside for a bit.

She stepped out into the cool air and breathed a sigh of relief. Then she searched in her pocket for her mobile and checked the messages. A few missed calls from Mac and a couple from an unknown number. Could be the bro-in-law. But if he didn't know anything about the baby, didn't even know that Mand was pregnant, she wasn't going to be the one to share her sister's secret.

She rang Mac. 'Hey Mac, what an afternoon. Although, I have to confess, it wasn't so bad for me as it was for Mand. Baby boy now, though. He's a wee cracker.'

'I'd no idea she was pregnant . . . you hadn't told me, had you?'

'Probably not. Mand and I haven't been on the best of terms for a while. Her call came completely out of left field. But all is well now. So if you want to reschedule our meeting I'd be happy to oblige.'

She heard him laugh at the other end – a sound that warmed her through and through.

'I could see you for dinner if you like.'

It hadn't been long since the muffin, but a decent dinner would be good. 'The Apartment would be great if we can get a table. Actually, forget that. Let's meet at Bella's. What's the time now? Six-ten. See you there at half seven if you don't hear otherwise.'

'See you then. And Viv, don't you go getting all broody now that there's a baby about!'

She laughed. 'Calm yourself. It's never going to happen. See yah.'

Seeing a new-born had definitely tripped a switch in Viv's biological cupboard, but not the one to make her broody. She had to get Mand to talk about what'd happened between her and Derek. He really had a right to know about his son, as much as it aggrieved Viv to allow him any rights at all. Should she ring her mum? She'd better speak to Mand before doing anything; this wasn't her story to tell.

As she returned to the ward, Viv detected the unappetising odour from food trolleys being trundled into wards, where unsuspecting patients were expected to improve, for God's sake. Mand was sitting on the edge of her bed with a man, who, on first glance, looked like the brother of a friend from Mand's high school days.

As Viv approached Mand looked up and smiled, not the sceptical smile that Viv was used to, but a warm welcoming smile that radiated from her whole face. 'You remember Viv?' Mand said to the friend.

'Course.' The man turned to face Viv and stuck out his hand to shake.

Viv shook the hand, trying to fit newly discovered pieces of a puzzle together. 'Hi. What bri . . .' Mand shot Viv a look which prevented her from finishing her inquiry. 'Good to see you again.' Viv said instead. She couldn't remember when she'd last seen Colin. Probably close to fifteen years ago. When he'd be in the car when his dad came to pick up Amanda with his sister Catriona on their way to play in a netball or hockey match. Viv smiled, recalling that every time they'd returned, Mand's games kit was still clean and their mum never seemed to catch on. After Viv and Manda's dad died, lots of families from their school took pity on them and there were always offers of lifts to and from school games and concerts. Colin and Catriona's dad had been a frequent taxi for Mand, but they hadn't been particularly chummy and Viv couldn't imagine why they'd kept in touch. Mand had become such a snob, and Colin and Catriona weren't on the right social radar to be included in the drinks parties or dinner rounds. Besides,

Derek would have forbidden it in his own manipulative way. Why was Colin here? Although Viv wasn't convinced that the man who stood before her was Colin. He was extremely polished.

Viv scolded herself for being unkind. Mand's attitude must be rubbing off on her. 'Look, Mand, since Colin's here I could nip home and grab something to eat.' Knowing that she had every intention of eating with Mac, but realising that the whole truth could, in the state that Mand was in, send her off on one. 'Anyway, you look as if you could do with an early night. How about I ring in the morning? I expect they won't keep you here any longer than they can get away with.' She watched as questions flickered over Mand's face as she decided whether to accept this excuse for a quick exit, but finally a look of resignation appeared and she nodded her consent. Once a big sister always a big sister.

'You're probably right. Col won't be staying long but we could do with a catch up.' She put her hand out to Viv. 'Thank you. I'm not sure what I'd have done without you.' She gripped Viv's hand and stared into her eyes. Viv knew that a message was coming through but she was not sure what. When she screwed up her forehead Mand shook her head ever so slightly and Viv nodded. The moment passed.

'See you in the morning.' Relieved to be off the hook so lightly, she waved as she backed out of the ward.

Released from duty, she was tempted to take a quick look at the crime scene in the next block, so followed the signs back to the teaching area; but there were too many people about for her to access the office again, and besides there was a PC standing at the other end of the corridor speaking into his mouth piece. Time to back off.

She jogged across the car park to the Rav and drove in a distracted haze home to the West Bow. She ought to ring her mum and everyone else who should be told about the baby, but Mand hadn't given her the go-ahead. One more day wouldn't matter.

Chapter Eighteen

When Viv reached her stairwell she sensed a presence. She glanced up through all six levels of landings and saw a figure leaning on the railings at the top, outside her door. She bit her cheek and prayed that it was Mac.

As she drew nearer, Mac said, 'How's auntie Viv?'

But he wasn't alone. Sal was sitting with her back leaning against the wall. Viv's gut tightened. She'd had enough drama for one day and couldn't face a confrontation any time soon. Although Mac's presence would counter the possibility of a real stooshie.

Mac and Sal spoke at the same time. 'You okay?' They laughed and Sal said to Mac, 'After you.'

'Sal rang and asked if I'd meet her for something to eat.'

Viv waved her hand. 'No problem. Just let me get in the door. We presumably haven't booked Bella's yet?'

'No, not yet. I'll do it now, though.' Mac took out his iphone and scrolled as he walked behind Viv and Sal up the hallway and into the sitting room. The room felt cramped. Mac was a big man, and although Sal was physically diminutive, intellectually and psychologically she definitely punched above her weight and having them both in her small sitting room was claustrophobic.

'Give me ten minutes while I clean up. She left them standing and went straight to the bathroom, stripped off and stood under a hot shower, hoping that when she turned the water off and wandered back they'd be gone, that they'd been a figment of an overwrought imagination. She winced as shampoo stung her eyes and thought of her sister's self-imposed situation. A baby on her own wouldn't be a picnic. Mand couldn't have planned it, could she? Was it actually Derek's? Viv stood wrapped in her towel as this question sank in. She dried herself and mused that that day she had been interrogated by Mac about her possible involvement in the death of a surgeon, then suddenly had found herself thrown into the drama of a birth. Two ends of the same cycle.

She knew that snooping around a death scene, criminal or not, wouldn't have gone down well with Mac. But still, she was curious that there had been a PC assigned to the corridor. They wouldn't do that unless the death was suspicious.

She pulled on clean jodhpurs and a shirt and in that moment decided that Manda's life was not her business. Time to back off worrying about things that she couldn't control. She padded through to where Sal and Mac were engrossed in a news report on TV. 'Any one hungry?'

They both turned to her and Mac switched off the TV. 'Let's go.'

Sal didn't speak but lifted her bag and slung it over her shoulder. Viv pulled on her boots, grabbed her rucksack and jacket and all three made their way to Bella's. Viv stared down at the wide pavement pock-marked by chewing gum, a Jackson Pollock in the making. They walked without discussing anything of consequence; there were polite enquiries about Mand and the baby and had the Royal got its parking sorted out? They were jus getting started on the new communal bins in the Grassmarket wher they reached Bella's bistro. They took a table by the window anc perused the specials board. A basket of mixed breads was laid ii front of them. No sooner had they each swooped on a slice wher two mobiles vibrated, one immediately after the other. Viv and Sa scraped back their chairs, and furrowing their brows, made theii way to the door. Mac shook his head, and scooped up anothei chunk of bread.

'Your car or mine?' Viv said to Sal when they had botl returned. Then she gestured to Mac. 'You coming? There's beer an incident at Sal's cottage.'

Mac counted out a bunch of notes and slipped them underneatl the salt cellar, calling over to Bella, 'Sorry about this, we have tc go.'

Outside on the street he caught up with them as they trottec towards Viv's car parked at the bottom of the West Bow. 'Wha now?'

Viv replied, 'We have to head for Doune asap.'

'Do you need me?'

Viv nodded. 'Always, Mac. Always.'

He shrugged. 'I'll take my own car. Sal, you happy to leave yours at Fettes?'

'Sure. I'll hitch with Viv. Follow us. There's been a fire at the cottage. Not looking like an accident. Moll's . . .' She shook hei head and jumped into the Rav.

Viv's knuckles were white with rage at the thought of anyone hurting the dog. Viv wasn't one for interference in the life of the underdog, but a real dog was a whole different thing. She put her foot to the floor and broke every speed limit until they screeched to a halt in Doune, forty-five minutes later. The roar of the diesel engine on the fire truck and the din of voices shouting were alarming. Viv racked her brain. Who would harm Sal? Or had this been meant for her?

They ran towards the house and heard barking. Brian stepped round from the side porch with Molly, straining at a leash. Sal dropped to her knees and cuddled Moll before tearfully asking what had happened.

Mac joined them. 'Here, everyone, slip these on.' He handed them little crime scene bootees and latex gloves. 'We wouldn't want evidence to be destroyed now, would we?'

Booted and gloved they wandered round the perimeter of the house. Viv handed Sal a torch, Mac had his own but it was almost impossible to see amongst the mature trees and bushes overhanging the drive and garden.

The cottage only had one ordinary vehicle entrance. From the fields anyone could get access if they were on foot, or on a very noisy quadbike. To the right of the house the land fell steeply towards the Ardoch burn. Someone could easily scramble up there, but why would they? The people in the old house shared an entrance with Sal, but had another drive on the Dunblane road.

Those gates were locked at night, and would require seriou. climbing skills to scale; besides they were entirely visible from the road so not worth the risk. At the bottom of the shared drive lay the Historic Scotland yard. Once a mill, its high perimeter walls and the Ardoch burn were deterrents to anyone trying to access Sal's from there. On the south side the quarry park followed the burn towards the Teith, which was an obvious escape route for anyone on foot, although with both rivers in spate not the easiest option Could someone just stroll up the drive and set the place alight?

Viv heard one of the fire officers shouting to the chief. So she made her way to where he was and waited for the other guy to join him. The flames had licked their way round the stone base of the conservatory and the heat had caused a few of the windows to shatter. But it couldn't have burned for long because she could still see the colour of the paintwork on the frame. It was blistered but not completely charred. Amateur stuff. The smell of petrol lingered on the gravel. The officer held up a small canister to his boss.

Viv stretched her hand out inquiringly, but the chief wasn't having it. 'And who might you be?'

Mac called from a short distance away. 'She's with the police!' Not entirely true for tonight's escapade, but she liked it when Mac stretched his principles. 'What have you got there?'

The chief grudgingly handed the canister to Mac and said. 'Generic kind of thing. Found in every garage. Was over the edge of the bank there.' He pointed to the steep banking leading to the Ardoch.

Mac replied, 'Generic it may be, but it'll have a production number on the base. If we find one locally that's in the same sequence, we'll have a lot less looking to do.'

The chief conceded and Viv and Mac strolled to the front of the house where the porch light made it easier to check for a number.

Mac patted his pockets. 'I've left my phone in the car.'

'I'll get it. Is it on the seat?'

Mac nodded to Viv, 'Front of the dash. That'd be great.' He continued to examine the base of the canister. Sure enough there was a number but not clearly visible in the poor light. 'Sal!' He shouted. 'You got a magnifying glass anywhere that's handy?'

'Sure, I'll get it.' She trotted up the steps of the front porch and in through the front door. Just about to step on an envelope she called back to Mac. 'Maybe have something here.'

Mac took the envelope by the corner and turned it over. Nothing written on either side. 'Who delivers a blank envelope?'

Sal shook her head. 'No idea. But whoever it was has been here in the last three hours . . .'

A piercing scream from the drive had Mac and Sal bolting in the direction of the cars. They found Viv sprawled on her back in a hawthorn bush. 'He went that way,' she yelled, pointing to the yard. 'There's no way out on foot, the river's too high.'

Mac tore round into the courtyard but couldn't see anyone and noticed all the outbuildings were closed up. He began checking the doors and spotted one with a loose padlock, which he approached cautiously. As he pulled at a latch, a set of headlights on high beam emerged from a lock-up on the other side of the yard, blinding Mac, and a vehicle screeched off at speed. He raced after it but failed to catch the registration.

He walked back to the entrance, where Viv stood brushing herself down with one hand, and holding up a phone in her other 'Think I got it. It'll be blurred but the techies will sort that. What a friggin' nerve they've got. Waiting around while all this,' she gestured at the fire engine, the police car and their own cars, 'is going on. They were here watching us when we arrived . . . He tried to lift me. Big mistake. I kicked his shins and punched wherever I could. Arse. I also bit his hand – again. That's if it's the same guy. I mean are we talking brass-necked sod or what?'

Mac seethed. 'They're playing a dangerous game now. The odd stone toppling, the odd hotel window breaking, is a lot different to torching someone's home. Whether it was occupied or not doesn't matter.' He shook his head and rubbed both his hands over his face.

Not familiar with this Mac, Viv said, 'Look at least we've got the reg or a partial on it. But are you seeing a connection to Sanchez as well? This is all a wee bit mad. By the way what's that?' Viv pointed to the envelope that he still held in his hand.

'Don't know yet. It was on the floor of the cottage. Nothing written on the front.' He took out a small bunch of keys and slid one of them along the edge of the envelope. He pulled out a single sheet with tightly spaced, hand written lines on one side. 'We'll read this when we go inside.' He put it back into the envelope and then into an inside pocket of his jacket. 'One thing, though. If they'd been intent on burning down the building they wouldn't have put a note through the door. So either this is from someone else, or we're dealing with someone who's as thick as pig shit.'

Viv raised her eyebrows.

'No point in looking at me like that. Let's try and get a proper description of whoever is throwing their weight around. The guy outside your flat was a huge athletic type who could have crushed you like a bug, so we don't want you going after him on your tod.'

'Give me some credit. There are ways to disable the mighty.'

He looked at her. 'Yeah, but only if you're prepared for them. You didn't expect that just now, did you? As for your training . . . never mind, it would be better if you weren't under threat at all, then you wouldn't have to be punching and kicking some stranger trying to abduct you. And by the way, always, I repeat, always, call for help.'

'What, you mean like just now when I screamed as he dumped me there?' She pointed at the hawthorn.

'So it was definitely a he and not a female dressed up as a he?'

'No, too bulky, hands like shovels. Just like the first time. I'm guessing same guy.'

The fire brigade had packed up and was beginning the precarious reverse down the drive. Inch by inch they steered the huge engine down the narrow path, the top of the driver's cabin whacking over-hanging branches, scattering twigs and leaves as they went. Once at the estate entrance they drove into the mill's courtyard, the only place for them to turn if they were not to reverse all the way to the main road. Viv, Sal and Mac waved them off then wandered up to the cottage and round to the conservatory It was a mess, but could have been a whole lot worse had Brian not been out doing his rounds. Another reprieve for the sneaky fox who'd recently killed four chickens up at the Old House.

Sal said, 'Thank God that Brian isn't the kind of bloke who sits on the couch nursing the remote. He's out and about in all weathers.'

Viv shared this sentiment.

Molly lay with her head on her front paws, her lead hooped over a tree root at the top of the garden the only obstacle to her running towards them.

Sal wandered towards her and she bounced to her feet expectantly. 'Why don't you guys go inside and find something to eat or drink and I'll give her a walk.'

In unison Viv and Mac replied, 'As if!'

'We'll all go. We could use the thinking time.' Mac shrugged. 'What the hell? I've done nothing I'd planned for this weekend and it'll soon be over.'

Viv glanced over her shoulder at him. 'Me either, but we've not been idle. Here.' She handed Mac her phone with the registration number on it, 'We should phone that in.'

Mac took the phone, 'That'll be the royal we.'

Chapter Nineteen

The sky had cleared to reveal a spectacular moon. They stepped over the stile into the field and strode out towards the riverbank with Molly running ahead, relieved to be off her leash.

'Interesting, that whoever they are, they seem to turn up when either there's only one person about, or no one. Makes me think they wouldn't take us on collectively.'

Mac cleared his throat, 'That doesn't make sense, Viv. On Inchmaholme there were lots of people milling about. In fact that rock could have damaged any one of us . . . Although I'm beginning to think that it was a fluke. There is every chance that the lump of masonry was placed back there by mistake and the mason forgot to mortar it in.' Mac shrugged. 'Still, not convinced by my own rhetoric.'

Sal sniffed and added, 'We still don't know who the target is. Let's see, there's been the falling stone, a broken window, the tyre – we mustn't lose sight of the tyre. Those all happened in the same area so that's the first connection. But the two attacks on Viv could have been meant for either of us.'

With every step Viv drew in another lungful of organic dampness. The whiff of mashed grass and the gurgling burn were definitely bugging her. A fox barked in the distance and Moll took off towards the noise. Sal whistled and after a wide sweep of the field Moll returned to heel. Viv hadn't been confident to let her go running off, and this was probably the first time since Sal's return that the dog had had a decent run.

'Who are our enemies?' Viv blurted into the moonlight.

Mac and Sal stopped and stared at her.

She stared right back. 'What are you gawking at? Well, we all have them. None of us has to dig too deep to find them. These attacks are determined. They're not just for a bit of a laugh. Okay so nobody died, but that needs to be qualified by 'yet' in brackets Basically anyone whose nose we've put out of joint, either recently or in the dim and distant. We'll have to think hard. Because the thing is, we may not even know that we've done anything wrong We, as they say, cannot give offence but people take offence as sure as the sun rises. And don't look at me as if I've lost the plot. Unless you've got better suggestions . . . Let's go through them one by one. You first, Mac.'

'You're mad. I couldn't begin to list the people who might have a grudge against me. There are hundreds and that's just the personal ones. Don't get me started on the professional crazies. My inbox is FTB with threats from nutters who'd like my head on a chopping block. But seriously . . .' He sighed. 'You are serious, aren't you?'

'Of course I'm friggin' serious. We've all had incidents in the last couple of days, and they could have been a whole lot uglier than they turned out. Now if I'm not mistaken; if these "accidents",' she signed inverted commas, 'had happened to anyone else, we'd have a team working out who the sods are.' She shook her head. 'You know what. Fuck this. I'm heading home. This country air is doing bad things to my brain.' She sank her hands into her pockets and stomped off towards the cottage. Mac and Sal were behind her while Moll ran ahead.

'Wait, Viv,' Mac shouted. 'We're all after the same thing.'

Viv stopped and turned. 'I know. But I need to get back to town.' She rubbed her hands roughly through her hair. The more the idea of fleeing burrowed into her mind, the more desperate she was to just get in the car and go. There was nothing she could do to help from here that she couldn't do from the flat. Besides if she went home they'd soon find out who the target was. Such a brazen attacker was bound to try again.

As she walked she threw over her shoulder, 'Well, let's start with the last three months. There's obviously someone, or maybe two people, who want us to sit up and pay attention. They've been willing to get themselves up to Doune, and maybe as far as the island. We mustn't forget that.' directing her comment at Mac.

'Sure we can't but . . .' Mac lowered his voice. 'Wait!'

Viv and Sal stopped dead and followed the line of his gaze. To their right, a large expanse of field led to the base of a hill, crowned by a small copse. Mac shook his head and kept staring at the copse. 'I thought I heard something coming from up there.' He pointed to the crest. 'Stay here and I'll go and take a look.'

Sal clipped Molly into her leash and rubbed the dog's ears. She and Viv stood awkwardly, as Mac strode off towards the phantom in the trees. Neither spoke, just watched as Mac's shadow fell, like a monster from an animation: huge, long and bulky, stretching way beyond human proportions.

Viv whispered, 'I think we all need a break from this. He's probably started seeing things now.' She smiled at Sal, but she didn't respond.

After a few minutes of silence Sal nudged Viv's arm. 'I think I've got an idea of who might be behind this.'

Viv swung round. 'But how?'

Sal shook her head and gestured to the cottage. Viv understood that she'd explain when Mac got back. But he'd gone from sight and they remained static apart from occasionally stroking the dog who was restless, tugging at her leash, eager to keep moving.

Eventually Mac emerged from the trees and strode back down the hill, nodding as he came closer. 'There's definitely been someone up there, they've left a half empty bottle of cider, and a few fag stubs. Could be a local seeking a bit of peace.' He shrugged. 'C'mon, let's get back.'

Sal said, 'Locals use this place as a retreat. I'm always finding little piles of fag butts and empties of one kind or another.'

Viv interrupted Sal, 'Sal thinks she's got an idea.'

Sal shrugged. 'It's only an idea. But a few weeks ago I got an email from a complete stranger claiming to be from a charity, encouraging me to set up a trust to help . . . Oh, I can't remember, orphans in Somalia or something. It didn't look kosher. It's not the first time it's happened and I thought it was, as you say Mac, some nutter. I ignored it. Don't know if I even kept it.'

It was Viv's turn to shrug. 'No matter, we'll retrieve that in a jiff.'

They approached the house and Viv, still itching to go home, knew she'd have to take a quick look at Sal's laptop before she left. Mac was a great investigator but IT wasn't his strong suit and it would be down to Viv to dig the email out from the ether. Sal was luckily not known for deleting info. Viv had experience of Sal's inbox, which was always choked. Even with a narrow time frame she was confident she'd get it done.

Viv chewed on the inside of her lip as she clicked on the keys, with Mac and Sal looking over her shoulder. Even if Sal had deleted it, an email was never lost, but some systems were more efficient at hiding, or encrypting them than others. As it turned out, Sal had deleted the message but she was able to identify other emails from the approximate date, so although it took Viv slightly longer than she had thought to retrieve it, it wasn't that tricky. With the message before her, she trawled through the endless numbers on the server whence it had come, and decided it was from the same server as the hospital. She took out her phone, scrolled, and found what she was looking for. 'Yes!' she announced. 'It's definitely from the same server as the others. So we're back to Sanchez' machine at the Royal. My bet's on the secretary and her chum, whoever he is. So that's where I'd go next.'

Mac coughed. 'I'm sure you would, Viv, but I think it's already way past the time for proper police intervention. We're not the Famous Five.'

This had Viv raising her eyebrows. 'What? And this isn' proper? Watch it, matey, or you'll be looking for another hacker.' She tossed her rucksack over her shoulder and headed to the door 'I've got to get back but if you should need more improper stuff doing, let me know.'

Mac started to reply. 'That's not wha . . .'

But Viv waved and closed the door behind her.

Chapter Twenty

Back in her own flat Viv changed into her PJs and buttered a couple of slices of bread straight from the toaster. She licked a trickle of butter off her fingers, sipped a waiting cup of hot chocolate, and dropped onto the couch. She lifted the remote, and idly flicked through the channels looking for something mindless. It was almost midnight and she couldn't find anything other than cookery programmes that was of any interest, and she knew she was only watching those because she was hungry. After a few minutes she took some deep breaths and felt the familiar tingle of relief flood through her body. The ping of an email arriving in her inbox woke her from what was the closest she'd get to a meditative state. Reluctantly she read the messages. Three had arrived at once, all from clients. This cheered her up. One message, a perceived emergency, had Viv grinning, and musing that all was relative in the world.

Gail, a friend she'd worked with a couple of times and whose hair appointments were irregular since she worked between Edinburgh and London, said, 'I've left a message on your landline, but I'm getting desperate. I know this is last-minute, Viv, but I've squeezed a place at the St Laurent show at Linlithgow Palace tomorrow night. One of my colleagues is sick. I look like a total tramp, and wondered if there was ANY chance . . .'

· This was the perfect excuse for Viv to get her scissors out. She replied asking where and when, not expecting an answer unti morning, so she was surprised when her inbox pinged again.

Gail's message read, 'OMG. Are you sure???? All of us, the meagre hacks, have been given accommodation in the most horrendous hotel on the M9, just outside Linlithgow. The broadsheets are somewhere more exclusive. We have to be there early evening. They have to search and tag us before we get bussed to the Palace. My hair looks nothing like the photo on my ID card so I'm sure they won't let me in. All manner of subterfuge going on; clearly a minor Royal planning to be there, otherwise they wouldn't be going to this kind of bother. Could you come to the hotel??? Do I owe you or what?'

Viv grinned and whispered to herself, 'Sure, but I could do with the distraction.' She hadn't registered the importance of the fashion show. Of course it was a real coup for the Scots to get Paris couture, and super-models from around Europe. And Linlithgow Palace was as spectacular a location as you'd get anywhere. She replied, offering a time in the late afternoon and requesting details of the hotel and room number. Time for bed. As she brushed her teeth she became aware that she felt lighter. She shoogled her shoulders, definitely less tight. Must be the idea of regaining some control.

She woke early, refreshed and keen to go for a run. The streets were quiet as she headed up Candlemaker Row, along Forrest Road and onto the Meadows. This was about as green as she could stand after a week in the country. At least here she had the choice to run on pavement or the equally hard, well-worn, gnarled, tree-rooted edge of the playing fields. She did a bit of both. After a full round of the north pitches she still had the energy for a bit more, so she crossed the road and jogged round the Links as well, finishing up with a sprint back down Middle Meadow Walk. In the forty minutes that she'd been out the traffic had doubled and she had to jostle for a space on the pavement.

The newsagent in Forrest Road caught her eye and handed her a *Scotsman* above the heads of a throng of blue-blazered Herioters queueing for crisps and sweets. Liberated by time on her own, she fantasised about industrial strength coffee and fresh croissants at Bella's. After a hot shower, she checked her inbox and read an email with details from Gail. Late afternoon was fine; she had plenty of time for research after breakfast. With the day free, she skipped up the hall, hoisted her jacket on and headed out the door. The Grassmarket was teeming with people. An overcast sky was clearly not enough to deter the early bird tourists on their way to the castle, or to visit Greyfriars' Bobby whose nose had been worn down by people touching it. What would the cowelled friars have had to say about such canine idolatry?

Still, although there were lots of them, tourists were usually in good spirits, especially Japanese groups, who were incredibly polite. By the time she'd reached Bella's she was grinning from ear to ear. It was like running the gauntlet of the paparazzi, only they weren't in the slightest bit interested in her. Every building in the

Grassmarket had had a famous visitor at some time in the past even the building that Bella rented had been host to many a body snatcher.

This morning, though, all Viv needed to do was breathe in th smell of heavenly coffee and plonk herself down in her usual sea by the window. She slipped her jacket over the back of the chai and laid out the newspaper.

Bella approached wearing a tightly wrapped full-length apro1 and a tea towel draped over her shoulder. 'How you doing, Doc' Been away?'

'Yep, fine, just back. Looking forward to some of that coffee o yours.'

'Anything else? Got a freshly made batch of almond croissants.'

'Sold! One of those and a large cappuccino.'

'Be right with you.'

Bella was a slim, dark-haired, brown-eyed darling who had n(idea of the effect she had on others. Which was of course why everyone adored her. The name above the door was never referred to, and so often when Viv said she'd meet someone in Bella's they'd look bewildered, since there wasn't such a place in the Grassmarket.

On page three of the newspaper was a headline for the fashior show at the Palace and under it three photographs of young womer in tartan, each looking as if they could do with a good meal. She snorted just as Bella arrived with her coffee.

Bella glanced at the photographs. 'There's been a lot of tall about that show. Apparently they're spending four million on it. A couple of limos with darkened windows have been round the market. Takes me all my time to brush my hair and my teeth, never mind all that palaver.'

'Four mill. Sounds obscene.'

'St Laurent's entourage are staying at the Caledonian. Security is mad on King's Stables, since that's where they're parking all their buses and cars.'

Although Viv had only been away a week or so she felt as if she'd dropped the ball. Aware that the show was going to happen, she'd not bargained on it being such a big deal. But now she could see that if Yves St Laurent himself pitched up, Scotland's great and good would be wheeled out to see him. The croissant arrived and Viv tucked in, flicking to the next page of the newspaper. Bit by bit, as the coffee reached the parts she needed it to and the croissant melted in her mouth, she felt herself returning to normal, whatever that was. There wasn't much news to inspire her so she satisfied herself with the crossword. Defeated three-quarters of the way through, she gestured to Bella for the bill.

Back on the street she stared at the sky. The cloud had lifted and the sun was making an appearance - summer definitely on its way. She had to remind herself that Edinburgh wasn't only a destination for festival aficionados, but drew people from all over the world, year round. She dodged a clutch of women who, judging by their hair tint, were Italian, their brightly coloured jackets and clashing scarves a breath of old European bravura. Viv loved living at the hub of the city and could sense its growing insomnia; like London or Paris, or New York, Edinburgh slept less and less. She approached her stair door, hesitated, then decided to nip up to the City Library to check a few newspapers and back copies of journals. Justified by her interest of 'know thy enemy', even if he had died of natural causes.

The librarians knew her, and were, as ever, incredibly helpful. Even when she gave them little to go on, they usually came up with some idea of where to look. Armed with ring-binders full of neuroscience journals, she went to the far corner of the room and dumped them on a huge oak table. With paper and pad at the ready she prepared to set down whatever had interested Prof Sanchez, and if he was as famous as Ger had made out, his name was bound to turn up within these pages. She spent an hour perusing the contents pages, then the index, for any mention of his name. Zilch. How odd. She went onto one of the computers and typed in his name. She'd already done this at home and very little had surfaced, beyond the conference that she'd seen on the notice board in the hospital. Same again. Zilch. Weird. Geraldine had used words like 'ground-breaking', and 'pushing the envelope' (a particular pet hate of Viv's); she might even have called him a 'genius'. Was Geraldine so smitten that she'd been conned? Viv knew to her cost how easily that could happen.

Love was an illness, where everything became super-distorted in favour of the lover. Suddenly they were 'just enthusiastic' and not the complete bore that, had anyone else appropriated the very same subject, would bring on a session of serial yawning. Had Ger been led a dance by this guy? His screen saver was surely a give-away. Viv thought of her own lovers. If she'd discovered that they had exes all over their screens, she'd have made loud noises. Ger couldn't have seen the photograph of his wife and girls. 'No way.' She said this out loud and was aware that a few eyes had strayed to her side of the room. 'Sorry,' she whispered to the man at the next table, who'd managed to raise an eyebrow. She'd obviously interrupted his nap. But he clasped his hands on his ample belly, and settled his bearded chin onto his chest— a sure sign that dozing was the only thing on his mind.

Frustrated, she returned the ring-binders to the Librarian's desk and headed over to the National Library. Its grand entrance and reading rooms with club silence reminded her of her PhD days. Hours spent perusing books, often up blind alleys that were irrelevant but fascinating. Once she'd scanned the catalogue and found Sanchez, she handed the man behind the desk a slip with her request. It would take a few minutes before the material was brought up from the miles of stacks that lay beneath the building, so she contented herself with a look at the exhibition of Jacobite letters and memorabilia.

The material that she'd requested also turned out to be a dead end. This Sanchez had a different first name. Andreas Sanchez must be related. How odd that there were two of them working in neuro-psychology in Edinburgh. Even more frustrated she headed back to the flat. If Stephanos Sanchez was that clever he'd be all over the journals. Her research had taken longer than she'd expected and there wasn't too much time before she'd have to leave to drive to Linlithgow. She'd made notes of the shenanigans of the last few days, some of which prompted her to email her solicitor, making clear that their system's protection wasn't up to speed. She also checked the address for the female she'd followed from Sanchez' office. Google had fantastic photographs of the big house and grounds in its hey-day. Until the nineteen eighties the house had been home to the Kingston Clinic, where early Nature Cure practitioners had treated patients who'd rejected orthodox medicine. The practitioners had been way ahead of their time, if the testimonies of the cured were anything to go on. The internet was completely moreish, and she had to drag herself away from reading about the history of their organic walled garden and hydrotherapy treatments. Sad that the gardens, tennis courts, and gym had all gone. At least converting the main house into chic flats meant it remained standing. The shabby accommodation of the secretary was probably still in its original state. Viv preferred it that way.

Viv gathered up her hair kit and tossed a packet of oatcakes into her rucksack – she might need a nibble.

Chapter Twenty-One

A lorry had jack-knifed on the roundabout at Newbridge, causing a snarl-up. Her patience tested, Viv drummed her fingers on the steering-wheel, and changed the radio station a few times. Eventually she settled for a Simon and Garfunkel CD. Her phone beeped, and she glanced at an email just as the traffic began to move. Sod's law; it would have to wait. When she arrived she could see what Gail meant by 'budget hotel'. Reception was busy and Viv looked out for signs indicating where the bedrooms were. Guessing that 209 was on the second floor she headed up the stairs. The management obviously didn't expect guests to use since its scuffed utilitarian paintwork would have been at home in a correctional facility. Narrow corridors could barely take the width of a suitcase; no space that could be slept on was wasted. She knocked on the door of 209 and it immediately swung open.

A female, not Gail, beckoned Viv in. 'You must be the hairdresser.' Dismissive.

Not a good start. 'Yep! That's me.'

'Gail's in the shower. I guess you can set up over there.' She pointed vaguely toward an area in front of a built-in wardrobe with a single mirrored door.

'Thanks. I'll do that.'

There were two single beds with matching purple covers. Still,

they were only here for an overnight and not much of that sh
supposed. The sound of running water ceased and in minutes Gai
stepped out of the bathroom in a tee-shirt and jeans.

With her hair dripping wet Gail rushed towards Viv as if sh
was going to kiss her, then remembering that that wasn't the kin
of relationship they had, she rubbed Viv's arm. 'Thanks fo
coming, Viv. My press photograph looks a whole lot different t
the way I've been looking recently. But you'll be able to sort tha
in a jiff.'

Viv hadn't seen Gail in a few months but was surprised at how
nervy she was.

The other woman waved and said, 'I'll leave you to it.'

Instantly Gail relaxed. 'Phew.' She nodded in the direction the
woman had gone. 'She was hoping for a room of her own and ther
I turned up. She's frosty. Thinks this is way beneath her.' She
glanced round the room. 'Fuck sake, it's beneath all of us, but it'
only for one night.' Gail pulled a tub chair over to where Viv hac
set down her cutting sheet. 'Let's get this chopped.' Gail showec
Viv a laminated card with an unrecognisable photograph on it
'One of those, please.'

Viv raised her eyebrows but said, 'No problem. How's Rod?'

'Persona non grata I'm afraid. Found a receipt. Christ, do the
never learn?'

'Could have been a gift for his mum, sister, cousin . . .'

'Or new girlfriend.'

'Ouch. How're you doin'?'

Gail grinned. 'Never going to be on my own for long, but for now, it's fine.'

'Really fine, or off-the-scale "Fine"?'

'Let's just say I'm keeping busy, otherwise I wouldn't have taken on this event.'

They had friends in common and chatted easily, catching up on people that one or the other had seen recently. It didn't take long for Viv to reinstate the look on the press card, and within forty minutes she was packing up her kit again.

'You fancy a drink before you head down the motorway again?'

'No, thanks. Not worth having even one these days. Besides you've got super-models to meet, and fashionistas to write about.'

Gail shook her head, 'Vacuous or what? But it pays the bills. I think the crowds are hoping Kate will turn up. As if! The Royal is much more minor that that. It's Yves they're worried about.' She handed Viv fifty quid and the deal was complete.

Chapter Twenty-Two

As she drove down the slip road and onto the motorway a vision of Manda and the baby ran through her mind. Should she? But no sooner had she reached 'should' than she decided against doing anything. Listening to Radio Scotland, she cruised down the M9. It was during this reverie that she noticed the strobe of blue lights approaching in her rearview mirror. The car drew up behind her, too close for comfort. It was unmarked but with a temporary light attached and rotating on its roof. She knew she needn't pull up for any car, even if they were police. She had a vague notion that as a woman on her own she wasn't obliged to get out of her car, but she was unnerved by their proximity.

She wasn't speeding, but she slowed and continued to drive. The car didn't back off. It got closer and closer until she imagined it hitting her rear bumper. She'd report this as harassment once she'd found out what they were after, but they'd have to wait until the next services at Linlithgow. She thought about ringing Mac, but her phone was in her rucksack in the foot-well of the passenger seat. She lunged for it, but swerved onto the hard shoulder. The car following reissued its warning with a siren blast. She was irritated and couldn't be arsed with this. What could they possibly have on her at this time of night? Everything was paid up, she hadn't been speeding, or swerving for that matter. They should be chasing out-of-control boy racers from Falkirk, but no, they were bugging her, when all she wanted was to get home to bed. She indicated at the turn-off for Hopetoun House, but they had other ideas, and speeded up on her inside to prevent her from entering the slip road. 'What the fu . . .?' This time she did have to swerve or they'd have put a serious dent in the side of the Rav. A high-speed driver in the outside lane tooted her a long loud warning as she straddled the lanes.

She swiped at a hair that kept falling over her brow. There was no way that a police car would do this, at least not with other drivers to witness their actions. Who the hell were they? She kept squinting in her mirrors but with reflecting headlights bobbing up and down it was impossible to see them. She made another attempt to reach her rucksack and this time caught the edge of the strap, but still couldn't grab enough of it to pull it onto the seat. She tried again and caught it, but as she did they tapped her rear bumper and she jolted forward, losing the bag in the process. Infuriated, she put her foot to the floor and hit her hazard lights. She'd draw attention to this caper one way or another. Some busybody was bound to report them. It occurred to her that they must want attention, otherwise why approach her this way at all. They obviously wanted to scare her, but why? Was this an arbitrary intimidation or did they know her? Was it actually her they were after? The next mile took forever, but she managed to retrieve her bag, although not yet her phone.

Viv considered the other incidents of the past few days and

decided that it was too infantile, too random, to be connected to the other attacks. Those had relied on someone watching the cottage Had these guys followed her from the hotel? She hadn't noticed anyone tailing her, but that didn't mean they hadn't been. It struck her that they always seemed to know when she was on the move Was her car bugged? That wouldn't account for them attacking her outside the cottage, unless it was she who was bugged. The most obvious thing was her mobile phone, an easy device to track if you had the wherewithal. She stretched again to retrieve her phone. He followers shunted into her rear bumper again and she cursed. They were able to see her, but she couldn't see them. Their headlights now on full beam, prevented her from even telling what kind of car it was. If only she'd managed to grab her phone.

It rang, which made it easier to locate. She'd jammed it into a pocket on her rucksack, the one specifically designed for mobiles By the time she held it in her hand the caller had hung up. And she couldn't see what the number was. The occupants of the car behind were willing to take a huge risk: the penalty for falsely claiming to be the police was a jail sentence. Between bouts of frustration and anxiety she tried to reason what they were up to. Since they hadn' hurt her so far, they must need her in one piece. Neither of the previous attacks had left her anything more than stunned and a bit sore.

She toyed with the idea of pulling onto the hard shoulder and remaining locked in the car. Would they attack her with other cars passing? It might be one way of getting a better look at them. Was it worth the risk? 'Think Viv, think,' she whispered to herself, thumping the steering wheel. 'You're not using your head. Think, woman.' Within a couple of minutes she'd be on the outskirts of Edinburgh where the traffic would increase; surely her followers were bound to back off then. She held her nerve, their headlights still menacingly close in her mirror, and as anticipated the traffic did increase and her attackers were forced to turn off their high beam. At the Newbridge roundabout, they drove along her inside again and prevented her from taking the main route to the Gogar junction. Instead she was forced to continue until they pushed her onto the city by-pass.

She still couldn't see them, only that there were definitely two of them. She stretched for her phone, and after almost losing the Rav to the hard shoulder again, she grabbed hold of it and pressed digit two, which was Mac's fast dial.

It went straight to his messaging service, so she screamed, 'I'm on the by-pass being harassed by people pretending to be cops . . . they're trying to force me off the road . . .' The phone beeped, the battery dead. Unsure how much of her rant he'd hear, she felt her panic rise. The car continued to tail her, still far too close for comfort. Viv flashed continually, hoping that someone would report the crazy behaviour to the real police. She began to snake over the central line back and forth, back and forth. The pursuers put their siren on but she was unfazed and continued her zig-zag progress. When she reached the slip road to Sighthill she put her foot to the floor as an articulated lorry was turning off. She just sneaked in front of him and rejoiced at the blare of his horn. At the top of the slip road she accelerated to the right on the roundabout towards Heriot Watt University. They'd probably expected her to go straight into town. Her ploy worked. When she'd gone full circle she returned to the city-centre route, and watched their tail lights ahead. She slowed at the next roundabout, her adrenalin pumping so hard she thought she could have a coronary. How could all that mad driving go unnoticed? Normally if you dared to step out of line you'd have an army of people on their horns or making gestures unfit for human sight.

Once her attackers realised that she wasn't in front of them what would they do? Unwilling to wait and find out she took a right into Wester Hailes and for a few minutes trawled round the scheme before heading onto the Lanark Road. It struck her that they could be waiting in the West Bow, but if she timed it right the Bow Bar would be spilling out its punters, and they wouldn't be able to touch her. She drove back, slowing at amber lights, and being more courteous than she would normally. When she arrived in the Grassmarket she circled but didn't see any sign of them Again unwilling to take an unnecessary risk, she dumped the car in a motorcycle bay at the bottom of Victoria Street, ran across the road through the throng of smokers outside the bar, and after fiddling with her entrance's dodgy lock, jogged up the stairs. With her super-strength lead lined door double locked and bolted, she leaned heavily against its panels and drew in a breath too great for her lungs.

Chapter Twenty-Three

She woke in the middle of the night, sweat-soaked and parched. She stretched for the glass of water and a pack of Paracetamol that she'd taken to bed, a just-in-case-measure. After gulping down two pills she fell back onto the pillow and eventually back into a restless sleep. The next morning there was no direction in which she could move that wasn't excruciating. Her head was pounding and her muscles objected so badly that she thought maybe a visit to the surgery was on the cards. She weighed up the pros and cons. Could she cut anyone's hair in this state? She decided she'd have a go.

She had one email from Karen, a client, and she shot back a reply saying she could see her later that morning, then had to twiddle her thumbs until Karen confirmed. Her inbox pinged and she read a message from Geraldine, requesting to meet up, which sounded urgent. She replied saying, 'no can do', but asked her to ring. Within seconds her mobile rang but the caller didn't speak. Viv waited and waited, then cut the call. She wasn't in the mood for a poor connection or intimidation.

It rang again and she cursed. Ger's shaky voice said, 'Viv, it's Geraldine. I don't know who else to call but . . .' The line clicked. Dead.

'Shit!' Viv tried to call her back but it went straight to an answering service.

Her landline rang and Viv snatched up the handset expecting Ger. 'Hi, Viv, it's me.'

'Mand! How are you doing? . . And the baby?'

'They're letting me home, could you come at 10.30 . . .'

Viv checked the time. It was nine-forty-five. ' Em . . . sure, I can do that.'

But Manda picked up the hesitation. 'Actually don't bother, I can . . .'

The dead tone.

'What the fuck is going on?' She yelled at the receiver.

Then dropping it onto the cradle she immediately picked it up again to check that there wasn't something wrong with it. There didn't appear to be. She tried to ring back but that also went straight to a message service. This was so typical of her sister, who was just too tight to unravel, volatile to the last. Viv wasn't in the mood to act as a salve for a woman whose hormones were leaping every which way. Frustrated, she flicked the TV on, scanned for a news channel, and waited for Karen or Ger to reply. The Scottish news had a story about Sanchez' death running in the red line at the bottom of the screen. She screwed up her eyebrows, unable to work out why they'd still be interested in such an old story, surely now dead in the water.

She increased the volume just as a familiar female reporter read 'There are a number of unanswered questions that Lothian and Borders . . .'

She shouted at the screen as if that would make a difference to the life of the reporter. 'Come on, Beeb, wake up! That's not what they're called now!' This was ironic, since Viv couldn't shake off the L&B label herself, but she expected higher standards of the BBC.

The reporter continued. 'The police are interested in speaking to Mr Sanchez' brother, Mr Andreas Sanchez, but he has, as yet, not responded to repeated requests to come forward.' Her emphasis hit a hopeful note on the 'as yet'.

Viv stood, staring at the woman, trying to read signs or keywords between the lines. What angle were the police taking? Should she call Mac again? He wasn't based at St Leonard's, the station nearest the crime scene, but he could still find out what was going on. Was he still up in the wilds of Stirlingshire? 'Unanswered questions' could mean anything, but surely concerned the death not being a 'simple' coronary as first reported. If she were having a coronary the last thing she'd describe it as would be simple. Nonetheless, something had made L&B suspicious, and although they hadn't mentioned murder she sensed it wasn't far off their radar. The brother was clearly a suspect, otherwise why would they be using the media to flush him out? Her inbox pinged again. It was Karen, desperate to take up her offer of a cut that morning.

With her rucksack flung over her shoulder, Viv took the stairs in her usual fashion and stepped out onto the West Bow, checking in both directions before she trotted down to the car. She gave a low air punch when there wasn't a ticket on the windscreen. It was a short but slow drive to Karen's, down the Cowgate, weaving past tourists trying to get a good look at the incongruent parliament building. She took a left, then an immediate right, underneath the railway bridge at Abbeyhill. The row of small, Victorian houses in Spring Gardens backed onto Holyrood Park. Dr Karen Anderson lived at number three with her parrot Pongo, and endless collections of socio-medical journals, press cuttings, or anything remotely connected to her research interests. She was always promising to have a clear-out, but, as far as Viv could tell, the piles only grew. When Viv rang the bell she heard footsteps shuffling up the hall, and imagined Karen's heavy hips rotating to avoid toppling the two hip height lines of piled papers and periodicals she had to negotiate before reaching the front door.

Karen was a woman of contradictions; a Canadian who had lived in Scotland for most of her adult life. Like many others, she came to study, fell in love with Edinburgh, and couldn't bring herself to leave. Viv cut her hair into a precise little bob, but Karen coloured it herself, too often and not well; consequently it was over-processed and rarely a consistent shade. Today, when she opened the door and peeked round, it took all of Viv's energy not to stagger back. Karen's hair was luminous pink, and with her spectacles pushed off her forehead it was sticking out as if she'd put a damp finger in a live socket. She must have picked up the wrong number of tint from the shelf, and trusted that the colour on the front of the box was actually the colour she'd turn out.

Karen's first words, 'Don't! I know, I know, I know. I've made a big mistake.'

Viv bit the inside of her cheek so that she wouldn't blurt out what she was thinking, but nodded her agreement. 'I didn't know that you wanted me to do colour.'

Karen's face contorted and her eyes filled.

Viv, seeing this distress, continued. 'But I'll nip back to the car. This is only my cutting kit.' She lifted her case.

Tears spilled down Karen's cheeks, and through a stifled sob she managed, 'Oh God, I'm supposed to be giving a paper at a conference at the weekend. Can you sort it? I look like Zandra Rhodes.'

Viv, taken aback that Karen, the epitome of an absent-minded academic, had even heard of Zandra Rhodes, thought unkindly, if only! At least Zandra Rhodes wore her lilac hair with aplomb. Karen, a rosy-cheeked, vertically challenged professor came nowhere close to avant-garde. Still wearing threadbare cheesecloth shirts and linen bags with drawstring waists as in her student days, style had never been on Karen's horizon. Although she was partial to the odd necklace – today's extravaganza was more like a breastplate.

'Give me five minutes and I'll check what's in the boot.'

'I'll leave the snib off; just come straight through to the kitchen.'

Viv returned with a selection of tints, one of which would hopefully correct Karen's woeful home-do. She pushed open the door and lifted her kit bag above her shoulder, and edged down the hall to the kitchen. Karen was sitting with her head in her hands.

'Don't you worry,' Viv said without conviction. 'I'm sure we'l manage to improve it.' Improvement was a relative term with wha she called the burst mattress look. After laying her large tarp on the floor and plugging in her hairdryer, she cleared a space on the kitchen table and set out tinting equipment on top of the sports section of a newspaper – since Karen was averse to any kind of vigorous movement, Viv thought this a safe bet.

Karen handed Viv a glossy sheet of A4 with a list of speakers' names; Karen's own impressive titles in bold advertised the keynote.

Viv rubbed Karen's shoulder. 'What exactly did you use? Did you keep the box?' It would be useful to know what she was up against in the correction department.

Karen rose and left the room, returning with a box with even brighter drips of pink obscuring the ingredients. Viv would have to guess from these remains what the base number had been and try to take it down a few shades, by neutralising the red with ash.

She gowned Karen up. 'Look, the best we can try for is a mid-brown. I'll have to counter the pink with . . .'

Karen held up her hands. 'I don't care what you do as long as it is no longer . . .' Karen grabbed at the frizzy locks, her eyes filling again, 'This!'

Luckily, although the colour was bad, there wasn't a great deal of hair to treat. Karen hadn't been blessed with thick tresses, so the application only took ten minutes. Viv crossed her fingers and prayed for a miracle cure. Karen was one of Viv's many clients who hated salons. She found staring at herself in a mirror for long periods too distressing. Having her hair done without this trauma was one of the main reasons Karen so willingly relinquished herself into Viv's trusted hands.

Not only did Karen collect journals and magazines, but she constantly entered, and won, competitions offering prizes. She also took every opportunity to complain eloquently, with very little reason. She'd told Viv that she'd even once complained about a squint label. The company had sent her a huge crate of replacements. Viv spotted three large boxes with a famous cute puppy on the side, and a couple of cartons containing Swiss bottled water.

Viv knew Karen and the house well enough to fill and switch the kettle on, 'Tea or coffee?'

Karen looked forlorn. 'I don't care. Either.'

Viv searched in the dresser cupboard and eventually found a coffee pot. 'It's going to be fine. You'll look lovely for the conference.' She lifted the sheet of A4 and read the location: Edinburgh University Medical School at the Royal Infirmary. Was it just her or were there too many things connecting her to the Royal? As Viv read through a couple of the abstracts, she was reminded how mind-numbingly dull she'd found rats and stats, mainly the stats, since she'd avoided the rats at all cost. The kettle clicked off. She'd never seen Karen look so down, and wondered if there was more to it than the hair disaster.

Viv tried to lighten the mood. 'Apart from having techni coloured hair, are you okay otherwise? You don't seem quit(yourself.'

Karen smiled. 'I'm fine, it's just that there'll be someone at th(conference who I haven't seen for years and I'd like to look m) best . . . not my absolute worst.' She snorted.

Viv grinned back, relieved to be doing work she felt relatively confident about. 'We'll make you look a million dollars.'

Karen snorted again and shot back, 'Now I know you're lying But I'm so grateful that you could come today. If I had had to slee[on this, I might have shaved it off or done something equally drastic.'

Viv sighed and, shaking her head, replied, 'Nothing's wortl doing that . . . by the way, are we about to have a world loo rol shortage?' She nodded towards the boxes. 'D'you know somethin(that the rest of us don't?'

Karen smiled. 'No. That's what happens when I'm bored. Th(first section of a roll wasn't double strength so I wrote to complair . . .' She covered her face with both hands. 'Oh boy, should I ge out more!' She shook her head and a rivulet of tint trickled dowr the side of her face. Viv jumped up and caught it with a tissu(before it ran under her jaw. The last thing Karen needed was (striped chin.

Although it wasn't really a question, Viv nodded emphatically 'Yes, you absolutely should.'

Karen leaned on the table and pushed herself up. Then, lifting a spatula from a jar of utensils prised open a high level cupboard, exposing shelves of packets of caramel wafers, 'See this. Complaining has its uses, but I'm running out of space.'

Viv gasped, 'That's a serious case of Diogenes syndrome. You know the guy who lived in a barrel? Well, you're creating your own barrel.' She smiled and let go of a deep breath. Viv, a big fan of Tunnock's caramel wafers, couldn't believe her eyes. 'I'd get through those in no time.'

Karen tossed her a pack of eight. Viv caught it and ripped it open. 'Fancy one just now?'

Karen returned to her seat by the table. 'No thanks, you carry on.'

Viv hadn't ever seen Karen eating, but there was always more than enough evidence that she spent a good deal of time doing just that, not least her growing waistline.

After discussing the work that Karen was taking to the conference, and munching her way through a couple of caramel wafers, Viv decided she could sneak into the Royal, pretending to be a delegate. She examined the hair. 'Yep. Almost there. We'll give it another few minutes then wash it off. It'll feel dull in comparison.'

Karen squealed. 'Thank God! Dull would be marvellous. I couldn't even answer the door to the postman this morning. So now I'll have to get myself to the nearest depot to pick up a parcel.'

Viv laughed. 'Another complaint?'

Karen shrugged. 'Could be.'

Viv gestured toward the sink with its mixer tap. 'Let's get that potion off. And see what's left of the pink.'

Karen staggered over, her breastplate almost tipping her into the sink.

'Mind how you go. That armour could drown you before we see what's happened to the colour.' Viv hadn't expected it to be perfect, but it was a vast improvement. She gently combed back the now warmish brown strands, knowing that they'd dry to a colour that would never earn a second glance. She took sections and snipped, sharpening the edges of Karen's short bob.

When Karen checked the finished result in the mirror her face cracked into a huge grin, exposing two rows of immaculate straight white teeth. 'Oh my God, how did you manage it?' Clearly overjoyed, but even a bit tearful again. 'It looks amazing. You're a complete genius. Let me write you a cheque.'

Chuffed, Viv told her the amount as she began to tidy away her tools. 'Where's Pongo? I haven't heard him.'

Karen blew into a handkerchief and pointed to the ceiling. 'Banished to my bedroom.'

Viv frowned. 'What's he been up to?'

'Nothing that you wouldn't expect a parrot to do. I kept saying shit, shit, shit when I washed off the colour, so guess what? I didn't want him repeatedly saying it while you were doing my repair work.'

Viv laughed and shook her head. With a kit bag in each hand she squeezed back down the hallway to the front door. There was no way that Karen could join her in the narrow space, until she opened the door and backed out, vacating the space for Karen to come and close it. Satisfied with a good job done, if it hadn't been for her load, she'd have skipped back to the car.

Chapter Twenty-Four

Viv switched the radio on in the car. The steady beat of the midday pips were ringing out. If she set off straightaway she could be at the Royal in time for lunches being distributed by staff busy enough not to notice someone carrying out a bit of reconnaissance. She parked at the fringes of the car park. Notices indicated where she should park for different lecture halls. She marched with purpose through the front doors, and followed the corridor round to where the teaching staff had offices. The whole place felt like a hotel, or a large office. Overhead signs for lecture theatres and seminar rooms were named after famous Scots. She stopped to read a noticeboard and spotted the flyer that Karen had just shown her; there was another sheet with more detailed biographies of some of the other speakers.

One of the speakers had a 'cancelled' sticker across his photograph. Viv's eyes widened as she realized it was of Stephanos Sanchez. His name hadn't featured on Karen's list and he certainly wouldn't be turning up to talk now. But Viv frowned. There was no note of condolence or mention of his recent demise. She screwed up her eyes and tried peel back the sticker to read text already blurred by red ink. It looked as if his talk would have been on trans-generational memory, a subject that Viv had read a little about and on which she would have been interested to hear more.

From this corridor she followed the signs to neuroscience. She jogged one floor up and found Sanchez' office with a blue police tape over its door. So, definitely not a heart attack. There were a number of people trickling back and forth, between their offices and what she assumed was access to their clinical work on the wards. No opportunity arose for her to check the door or nip beneath the tape. But at least there was no longer a police presence.

The young female doctor, with the stethoscope that looked like a fashion accessory, came out of her office opposite to Sanchez'. She glanced in Viv's direction but was busy fitting her ear-phones in and didn't acknowledge Viv's presence. She walked towards the double doors at the end, exited and turned left. Viv followed and soon found she was leaving the teaching area and entering the hospital's clinical wards. She didn't have any purpose there and decided to retrace her steps, but just as she was about to push open the doors into the research department she glimpsed Sanchez' secretary, or at least the female whose big glasses and hair were unmistakable. Viv, too far through the doors to retreat, decided to carry on and nodded at the woman. Her look of surprise and confusion interrupted the conversation she was having with an orderly and she stared as Viv continued on her way. To where, she had yet to decide. Once through another set of double doors she hesitated, counted to sixty, and peeked back through the windows in the top of the door. She regretted it, as the secretary had resumed her conversation with the orderly. The orderly was facing in Viv's direction, and the woman made such a face that the secretary spun round. Viv stepped back and took off at a pace. She hadn't gone far when she sensed that someone was on her tail Glancing round she saw the secretary, with one shoe in each hand keeping a safe distance, but with a look on her face that left Viv in no doubt that she wasn't in the least happy to see her.

In order to avoid a public confrontation Viv needed to get herself to the busiest area of A&E, then she'd be able to lose her Acres of corridors with misleading overhead signs took her out of neurology, into oncology, urology, and other 'ologies' that she'd never heard of, until eventually she burst through a set of doors into a large glass foyer, like an atrium, with lots of people milling about, queueing for coffee, soothing children – the world and his wife were represented there. Viv ducked into the back of a group that looked like a school football team, complete with spotty-faced youths munching crisps and swigging Irn Bru, shouting and laughing uproariously at nothing that anyone but them could find funny. It was a risk to walk with them, because if they noticed, she was bound to become an object of ridicule. Eventually they made their way to the exit and as soon as the doors hissed open and she hit the cool air, she bolted along the side of the building and round to search for the Rav in the far car park.

Once inside the car she sat catching her breath and wondering what the hell the woman was doing following her. But what the hell was she doing letting her? Why hadn't she stopped and questioned her? Mad, she was mad. 'Idiot!' she banged the steering wheel. If anyone knew anything about Sanchez it was bound to be the secretary. She started the engine and cruised round to where she'd exited the building. There was no sign of the woman anywhere. Viv decided to head home.

As soon as she left the hospital grounds she thought she'd take a left up the narrow road that ran alongside the estate wall of the house with the stable block where she'd last followed the secretary. Thinking that she'd do the same as last time and leave the car on the main road and jog back she was alarmed when a dark car travelling at speed behind her bumped into her back end. She was shunted forward, before the car sidled up on her inside and forced her into the lane where a filter turned green and she had no choice but to swing right into the drive.

More angry than she'd felt in a long time, she stopped, slammed the locks on, and sat staring straight ahead until a fist banged on the window.

'Fuck off,' she yelled, giving in to her frustration. She stretched for her phone, not hopeful but needing to check. It was still dead. She pressed nine, nine, nine and got through to a police operator. Just as she was beginning to give her location she caught a movement to her right and quickly pulled back as something long and hard was swung at the side window. That was the last she remembered.

When she came to, she immediately wished that she hadn't. A searing pain in her temple prevented her from opening her eyes properly. When she did manage to look out, it was under blood-encrusted lids. Lifting her right arm up to assess the damage was impossible. The piercing agony of her shoulder as she tried to raise her arm to her head made her yelp. She tried with her left hand and recoiled when her fingertips encountered a sticky lump the size of a creme egg. She was slumped on a concrete floor inside a sort of barn, propped up against a wall. Her butt and all her other extremities were numb. She tried to push herself up but there was no way her shoulder would allow it and she screamed out as pain ripped through her again. She allowed one good eye to adjust to the darkness. The edge of a window frame on the wall farthest away was about as much detail as she could make out.

After a few moments of blinking she began to trace the outlines of ugly, rusted, gardening machinery. Major obstacles: like over-sized unloved toys that she'd have to circumnavigate to reach any view of the outside world. The window let in a sliver of light, as if it had a shutter or a curtain drawn. She rolled onto her better side and tried to stand but nausea rose up her throat and she stopped until the bile subsided, then tried again. A cold sweat and excruciating pain compelled her to take tiny movements. Bit by bit she'd find a way of becoming upright and getting out of here.

As she recovered her senses she remembered that she'd been doing someone's hair. How long ago was that? She couldn't have been unconscious for that long, could she? The pain in her head was like nothing she'd experienced before. For a moment she wondered if she was alone. The last time she'd woken in the dark like this she'd been surrounded by a group of frightened women, each one more terrified than her. This was no container and the earth didn't seem to be moving. She thought she could hear the odd car engine, but nothing close by. Was her imagination playing tricks? The pale light coming through the window was yellowish, artificial, not moonlight.

She made another attempt to get herself up, but her head began to swim and she felt she would pass out. She lay curled up in a foetal position and worked on her breathing, mustering what was left of her resources before crawling toward the wall with the window. Only twelve inches wide by about twenty-four inches tall, she'd gotten through something that size when she was at uni, but then she was without any injuries. She blew into cupped hands, then continued scraping her knees over the concrete, and pulling herself towards the window. Only when she was lodged below it did she stare back into the gloom of the barn and realize she'd left a position right next to double wooden doors.

The window didn't have a shutter, but was covered in layers of cobwebs with mummified spiders and insects. She had no intention of clearing an arachnid graveyard anytime soon. Her first attempt to hoist herself up the wall made the nausea return, but she swallowed and pushed herself until she could squint through of the edge of the window with the least web build-up. The insipid glow from a street lamp way in the distance gave her some bearing. She visualized the courtyard outside the secretary's house, believing that she was in the old stable building adjacent; she imagined the window was facing away from the courtyard toward the big house. But she couldn't see any building, only the shadows on a lawn-like-surface, cast by some odd shaped trees. There was little more to give her guidance, but the idea of a street lamp somewhere near by was reassuring. It was a cloudless sky with a full moon.

Viv lifted her arm again, testing how high she could get it without shrieking in pain. She raised her elbow as high as her shoulder, before she dropped it carefully. She patted her pockets. They'd taken everything except a couple of partially used tissues. Inside the heel of her boot she kept an emergency pick, like a hairgrip, only tougher. It was some consolation that they hadn't thought to strip her of her boots. At this point she'd no idea how it might come in useful, but it was all she had and it could become a weapon. With two against one she'd have to be sure of escape before hurting one of them.

Slumped against a damp wall built of large concrete blocks, she shivered, unable to feel any sensation in her feet or the ends of her fingers. To remain overnight in this place would leave her seriously cold. She must keep moving. She scrunched her fingers, blew on them, and stamped her feet. Taking deep breaths in order to blow on her hands she thought she could smell the sea, but warned herself that the stressed mind could play weird tricks. She slid down the wall and crawled back round the old machinery towards the doors. The hinges were robust, industrial things that would take more than she could give them at present to break away from their fixings. She tried pushing against them but there was little give. There must be a padlock or a serious bolt on the other side. If she got to her feet again, she might be able to spy something through a tiny split in the wood near the top of the door on the right. Hand over hand she walked herself up the door. Viv was quite tall but the split was at least ten inches above her eye level. And with an army of stonemasons resident inside her skull, it was a stretch too far. She slid down the door and crouched hugging her knees and rocking from side to side. She'd have to find a way of staying awake through the rest of the night. No idea how long she'd been unconscious, she prayed that daylight wasn't too far off.

In the state she was in, there was little she could do to get out of the building, so she resolved to garner her strength until her captors returned, when a bid for freedom would be her only choice. Surely by then Mac would have picked up her call. Even if he hadn't got the message, there'd be a missed-call registered. A tarpaulin lay scrunched up in a corner and she sloped towards it. It would prevent the damp from seeping up her trousers even if it didn't exactly keep her warm.

Try though she had to stay awake she must have dozed on and off until sunrise, and she woke feeling more stiff and in more pain than she remembered from earlier. The building wasn't exactly light, but her sense of foreboding that came from the darkness had lifted, and she was more able to concentrate on a plan. She skulked back over the floor to the biggest of the machines, of which there were three. One, the body without its engine, an ancient Massey Ferguson tractor, another a large flat frame with spikes sticking down towards the floor, a harrow of some kind, and finally a lawnmower, the type with three gangs of rotating blades. Eac piece was seriously rusted. She had a go at one of the bolts on th harrow. Not a chance of shifting it without any sensation in he hands, and the others looked in even worse condition. She stoo and relying on the machines for support she made her way back to the window. This time she did clear the cobwebs and wiped at th filthy glass. No artificial light now, but no matter, the sky wa becoming brighter by the minute. She thought she heard the se again and this time she felt convinced, because odd shadows cas across the area in front of the tiny window belonged to a row o hardy, stunted, sea-buckthorn trees, the type that you'd find by th beach. 'Shit! Where am I? This isn't Liberton.' She thought o Shirley – maybe she wasn't such a loony after all.

There was nothing else to see but mown grass, tufted san dunes and a blue sky; neatly mown grass, in fact it was fairway She was on, or at the edge of a golf course, which could mean Eas Lothian. She tried to see to the right and left, but the fairways wer nestled in the shelter of dunes and she couldn't see the ocean. Nov when she heard waves she didn't tell herself off, but used th image of them gently breaking onto golden sand to improve he mood. She wasn't much good in the mindfulness department bu she had to try. She began tentatively to jump up and down, but th army in her head soon woke up and protested, so she skippe gently and chanted, 'Every day in every way, I love my life'. Witl each round the army protested, but not so loudly. This got he circulation going and eventually a tingling sensation crept into he hands and feet. She was mid skip and chant when one of the doors shook. Her belly lurched but she continued, on the basis that you should never let the enemy know how worried you are, and it is difficult to believe someone is worried if they are skipping and chanting.

It took a few minutes for the person on the other side to release the bolt and swing the door open. Viv didn't hesitate, and with her head down she hit the guy with her left shoulder. He staggered back, more from surprise than her strength, but managed to grab hold of her jacket and swing her to the ground. Pain shot through her shoulder and she almost threw up. But rage spurred her and she rolled over, got back to her feet and ran at him again, screaming at the top of her lungs. This time he grabbed and wrenched her head back by her hair. She screeched again, and swung for his masked jaw. The impact was enough to set him off balance so that she could catch him by the neck. She stamped on top of his foot while elbowing him in the solar plexus. Her attacker was bigger than she'd hoped and fighting back made him more determined to flatten her again. He swung a double hander at the side of her head and connected. She went down like a rock and didn't move.

Playing dead would buy her a little time to think what to do next, but he kicked her hard in the back, all the while cursing in Spanish or Portuguese. He heaved her onto her back and stood towering above her. Next, in what appeared like an act of defiance, he ripped off the mask and stared at Viv as if she should know who he was. She did have a flicker of recognition but couldn't place him.

He yanked her to her feet and hauled her back into the shed shoving her back against the Massey Ferguson.

The pain was agonising and she bit her lip, drawing blood. Then she shouted, 'What the fuck is it that you want?'

To her surprise he spoke in perfect English. 'Equity.'

She was flummoxed. What could he mean? 'Equity? What's that supposed to mean? D'you mean political, economic, sexual or what? And how the fuck do you think I can get it for you?'

He stood almost a foot taller than her, at six foot six inches, his arms folded, his feet apart. What she saw was over-compensation. It was excruciating for her to look up at him. Her vertebrae felt jammed into her neck and she moved towards him in an attempt to force him to step back. It didn't work. He held his ground. She spat at him. Viv hated spitting more than anything, apart from a guy trying to intimidate her by standing in her personal space.

He didn't move. 'Nice. Lady-like.' Sarcasm dripped off his lip as Viv's saliva trickled down his leather jacket. Even she was disgusted by what she'd done, but not so much that she couldn't concentrate on what her next move could be. As if he was reading her mind he said, 'Don't even think about it.'

'Fuck you! You think I'm in the slightest bit worried about etiquette with this cracker.' She pointed to her throbbing, bloody head.

He shrugged. Which did nothing to pacify.

'Okay. So who the fuck are you? And what makes you think I

hold the key to "equity"?'

He seemed unable to contain his anger. 'You did nothing. Nothing for her. Nothing for the family. Nothing. And yet you got it all.' Flecks of white foam gathered at the corners of his mouth. Never a good look.

Viv was confused. 'Wait a minute, who are we talking about here? And what was I supposed to do that I didn't?'

'You know what I mean.' His voice was cultured, and although not menacing, it had an aggressive edge. 'The solicitor told you we'd contest it.'

Viv racked her brain for the last time she had seen a solicitor. She shook her head painfully as if this would bring something to light. She hadn't seen one for at least two, getting on for three years. 'Oh, my God. You mean Dawn?'

At the mention of her name, he drew his shoulders up, and gave the slightest of nods.

Viv sighed, trying to calm her indignation. 'I don't get it. You can't have done all that you have,' she pointed to her wounded head, 'over Dawn's legacy. You must be mad . . . Who are you anyway?'

He took a step towards her, leaving less than a foot between them. Bad move on his part. Viv, quick as a flash, raised her knee and connected all her rage with his groin. She watched as, in slow motion, and with crushing disbelief on his face, he curled up and dropped to the floor. She darted to the door and out towards the dunes. She glanced left, then right. If she could make it to slightly higher ground she would get her bearings. Out to sea she saw Fidr nearby and the Bass Rock, in the distance to the south. She ra north-east along the fairway knowing that eventually she'd com to Gullane or Aberlady.

If she hadn't been in so much pain she'd have enjoye trespassing on such magnificent spongy grass. She'd no idea wha time it was but the sun was up and she was amazed that ther wasn't any activity on the course. She'd played a few in Eas Lothian but didn't recognize this fairway, surely a par five judgin by the distance she was running. On a hole like this she'd hav been into double figures.

When she reached the next tee she spotted a litter-bin emblazoned with a crest and, 'the nineth' written on its side. Thi hole would likely be the furthest from the clubhouse. After a quicl poke around inside the bin she found a broken pencil with Knight something embossed on it. Another clue, but needn't mean she wa actually on Knightsfield. She smirked. If it turned out to be th case it was the most misogynist course in Scotland, so sh wouldn't exactly be welcome in the clubhouse if she did eventuall find it. To the left of the tee she climbed another slight but rougl incline where she'd get a better view inland. She looked back nervous of her attacker's pursuit, but there wasn't a soul around What was going on? Knightsfield was one of the most famou courses in Scotland and with such exorbitant fees she imagined i being played round the clock.

'Think, Viv. Think.' Why would it be empty? The only reaso

she could think of was that they were preparing for a tournament. Then she remembered seeing an advert on TV for a memorial championship. A grand building with windows facing out over the course was a good bet for the clubhouse. It sat way in the distance; she was as far out as she could be. To its right a bank of trees shielded a row of houses with red pan-tiled roofs. She had to decide which buildings it would be best to approach. She didn't want more hassle than she'd already had. There must have been a reason for him to take her to that particular shed. She continued in the direction of the grand, Edwardian, two-storey building. She'd reached the green of the eighteenth when she heard the gunning of a machine. She watched as a man on a gang-mower reversed out from a series of smart new wooden barns in the trees, and made his way down one of the fairways.

She shouted, 'Hi there!' But he didn't respond. With ear defenders protecting him from the racket of the diesel engine, he was oblivious to anyone around. She tried again, this time waving her arms as high as she could bear to. She got within twenty feet of him before he cut the engine to a lower rev.

He hauled the defenders off his head. 'What . . . the hell . . . you shouldn't . . .'

She interrupted him. 'But I am, and I need your help. Where will I find a telephone?'

He jumped off the machine, and staring in disbelief at her blood-encrusted face, gulped back any further protest and pointed to a small building to the side of the main one. He walked ahead of her without speaking but gestured for her to follow. He took out a set of keys from his pocket and let them in the side door of wha turned out to be the professionals' shop.

He pointed to a telephone on a shelf behind the counter. 'Help yourself.'

When she reached for the handset she began to shake uncontrollably and misdialled. Her second attempt got her straigh to Mac.

'Where the hell are you? I've been trying to reach . . . '

She shouted into the phone, 'I'm in the pro shop at . . .?' She glared at the grounds-man.

'Knightsfield.'

She nodded her thanks. 'Knightsfield. Knightsfield golf course in East Lothian.' Her voice began to crack. 'Just come . . .'

'I'm on my way.'

No sooner had she put the receiver back into its cradle than the door swung open. Her very unhappy assailant, puffed out and sweating profusely, propped his hands on his hips and gestured to the man who'd let her in, to leave.

The grounds-man hesitated, but after the other man's aggressive nod towards the door, he edged out. A digital clock on the telephone confirmed the time as five past six. No wonder the course was empty.

'What now?' she said.

'Well, I was hoping I'd be able to make you see my point of view.'

The door opened again and a woman, Sanchez' secretary from the hospital, stepped in, pushed the snib on the lock, and stood with her back against the door.

'What exactly is it that you want from me?' There was no point in fannying about. She couldn't face another beating. Her head was still thumping like a bass drum and her shoulder was beginning to seize up. The secretary looked as if she was about to speak but the man shot her a warning glance.

He continued. 'The land. You got the land.'

'Who are you exactly?' Viv was intrigued. How did they know who she was? And how could they know about Dawn? Dawn had always been cagey about her friends and family. She recalled the meeting with her solicitor when he'd revealed what Dawn had left to her. She'd thought at the time that Dawn hadn't left her all that she had without some ulterior motive. The solicitor had said the family were unhappy about the will. But he had added that Dawn had made the whole thing watertight and that most families were unhappy about something and not to give it another thought. On that advice, since she'd never met the family, and knew how much Dawn had hated them, she'd disregarded the family's feelings about the legacy going to an outsider. Viv was grateful for having a significant nest egg to fall back on, but she had no inclination to dip into it. In fact, most of it had gone into trust, so her access to it could never be immediate.

He ignored her question.

Viv stared at him and nodded. Determined to goad him, she

ignored her own discomfort at receiving the legacy. 'I think you'l find that I got everything that she possessed. But none of it was a my bidding. If she wanted me to have it and was adamant that th family got no part of it, she had a message. So what did you eve do for Dawn, or not do for her, to make her react against you? An when I say you, I really mean your wife, since you're not famil any more than I am.'

His head came forward. Viv knew the longer she spoke th more chance she'd have of the troops arriving.

He cleared his throat. 'Dawn always said you didn't want to b part of the family.'

This was news to Viv, since Dawn had never invited her to an family events, claiming that she would hate them. Although in th early days she'd said that she didn't want to share Viv with anyon else, especially not her crazy relatives. Viv had heard this as th excuse that it was.

'We'd like it back.' The edge to his voice sharpened and th muscles in his jaw twitched.

He and the secretary kept glancing at each other. Viv wondere what their relationship was. Could she be the woman on th screensaver? She must be, otherwise she'd have done something t change it. And what about Geraldine? What part had she played i this? Was she simply used in order to get close to Viv? Surely h needn't have gone to such lengths.

'And who exactly is "we"?'

He stared, his dark eyes fixed on her. 'The land belongs in th family.'

'Yeah, got that. But who are you?' As she said this something clicked inside her brain. 'Oh my God, you're . . .wait a minute 'til I get this right.' She paused and looked. 'But you can't . . . you're Sanchez? Shit! And which sister are you married to?'

He flinched, which was all the confirmation she needed. So he was Sanchez. But who the hell was the dead guy in his office? Then it struck her that if this pair were responsible for his death, they'd have no qualms about silencing her. Although if money and land was their goal, it was in their interest to keep her alive. Her best hope was to keep them talking. They'd first want to secure what they were after, but in order for that to happen, which it never would, but in theory, they'd have to get to her solicitor. This was a leap too far. For now she should focus on warding off any more injuries. Some serious negotiating lay ahead.

Dawn used to joke about her mother being like Mrs Bennett, always worried about how to marry her daughters off to wealthy men. Consequently, Dawn hadn't come 'out' to her family, making the excuse that, as Catholics, they wouldn't understand.

'Okay, say I don't want the money or the land and am willing to give it to the family, who actually gets it? Are you going to split it between the other sisters and their husbands or partners?'

A look of disgust swept across his face. 'You're mad. You think we'd go to all this trouble for the others. We have plans.'

'Who's "we"?'

He hesitated, but didn't take his eyes off her.

She persisted. 'Plans to do what? Because people like you are never going to be satisfied. That's the thing about jealousy, it's insatiable. The more you feed it the more it wants. Look at you. Look at all the things you've done to get to this place in your head. But if you are who you say, you'll already know this.'

This was no way to keep him calm, but she was on a roll and enjoying herself. The more she thought about what they were up to the more her fury rose. 'You've clearly invented a sense of entitlement. You're no more entitled to Dawn's legacy than I am. Why should I give it up? If you had been given it, would you?'

He flexed his fists and took a step forward. The woman's eyes widened. She'd obviously been reconsidering, but his answer looked as if it was coming in the form of another punch. Viv swallowed. There were many possible weapons around her, not least a golf bag full of clubs on her immediate right. She stepped towards them.

'In your dreams,' he sneered. The gang-mower started up, and Viv's heart sank at the sound of the engine retreating.

Viv could smell her own anxiety. Her armpits were soaking but she distracted herself by thinking how ugly and contorted his face was with aggression. But now was the time to think about a strategy for surviving. The expression on his face didn't engender any faith that she would emerge unscathed. He rubbed his crotch. This set off a tiny alarm bell inside Viv's head.

'She's not saying much,' she blurted out, trying to distract him from whatever instincts were rising in him. God alone knew what his next move would be.

He wasn't biting and grabbed Viv's wrists. She held back her reaction as his skin twisted hers. He pushed his face into Viv's discomfort zone, and she felt his disgusting breath on her cheeks and kicked out at his shin.

'Bitch! If only I'd managed to sort you on Friday night.'

'You'd what? You'd have killed me, then what? Because you sure as hell won't get any legacy if I'm dead. Your only hope at the moment is to keep me alive until Tuesday, when my solicitor will come back from the weekend. Even then he was the one who persuaded me not to give you anything in the first place, so why would he now? Besides the money is in trust and the land is leased. Nothing would happen quickly.'

He rubbed his crotch again. And with his eyes screwed up he sneered, 'Shut your filthy mouth. You think that we haven't thought any of this through? Well you're wrong. My secretary here.' He gestured condescendingly with his head towards the woman. 'Will witness to your signing a . . .'

Viv swallowed and interrupted him. 'Not on your fucking life!' Proud of the depth of her own conviction she was ready when he took her right arm and twisted it up her back. A searing pain shot through her bicep. 'Bastard. I don't get it. You're well known, well admired in your field. Why would you risk all of that for what I have?'

'Because-it-doesn't-belong-to-you. It belongs in the family.' He stretched out the words, and pulled a little sharp scalpel from his inside pocket and held it up in front of her face.

Still unable to let it go, she countered, 'But you know that's no true. It does actually, legally, belong to me. That's the way Dawı wanted it. I've no idea why she wanted it that way, but she didn' want the family to have any of it. So why was that?'

He pushed her arm up her back and transferred the scalpel to thı hand that was holding her wrist, and it nicked the side of her neck This time she did squeal. Anyone this consumed by jealousy haı lost their sense of reason. The intensity of his belief distortec everything. He could no longer see sense. Jealousy is known as thı hungry emotion for a reason.

'Her filthy habits got her involved with people like you. Peopli who used her for who she was and what she had.'

This came completely out of left field. She hadn't considerec that his motivation was homophobia.

He continued. 'She had no idea what you were after. But knew. I've seen your girlfriend's accounts. You're a serial thief Wheedling your way into women's lives and stealing their money.'

Viv was mocking. 'You're fucking nuts. I had no idea wha Dawn had. She was never generous with anything, except her sarcasm.' This was the first time that Viv had said this aloud She'd thought it many a time but saying it gave it a differen quality, power, which spurred her on. 'You know what I think? think she hated you all. She hated you all enough to do what shı did, to set you against each other. What else could she have mean by it? She knew I didn't need her money. And I certainly had nı idea about Sal's.'

'Liar! Liar! You're a twisted liar!'

Viv tried to yank her arm out of his grasp but he had her locked and now the scalpel was perilously close to her jugular. She risked, 'That's rich coming from a sociopath like you!'

The secretary, dressed for a day on the hills, with waterproofs and a scarf, was clearly overheating. She loosened her zip but he threw her another warning look.

Viv turned her head towards the woman. 'You'll get nothing out of this. You do realise that, don't you?'

The woman's eyes flickered between Viv and Sanchez. The more Viv could plant doubt, the more likely the woman would be to turn against him. Whatever he'd promised her, there was no way he'd follow through. Viv had to make her understand this. 'Surely you can see that you'll never get away with this. He and his screensaver wife will be the only people who gain. You're just a pawn.' Viv, lying her pants off, because he would never get anything not least over her dead body.

He punched Viv in the side, where she had a not-so-old injury. She crumpled and felt bile rising in her throat. She swallowed furiously, unwilling to throw up over the plush carpet with its insignia of repeating knights with their bows pulled back. Well brought up to the last.

She could feel and smell his rank mouth close to the side of her face. It triggered a memory. Nothing good. She tried again to pull her arm away. He darted his free hand between her thighs and grinned, exposing perfect white teeth. She pulled her lower hal

away and to her own astonishment gifted him with a Glasgow kiss

She'd connected her forehead with his nose and it was enough to

cause a trickle of blood to escape onto his lip. He grinned again

his face reminding her of Jack Nicholson on a bad day. Suddenly

he started roughly pulling at the zip of her trousers. She kicked and

elbowed and although he dropped the scalpel, her aggression

seemed to make him more determined, frenzied, aroused.

'Bitch! Hold still!' He fumbled with his own trouser zip. 'I'm

gonna give you just what you need.'

This man had lost the plot. Then out loud, 'Like fuck you are.

She punched his jaw beneath the chin. His teeth clashed and he

yelped. Viv stopped abruptly with her fist in mid-air, and glared a

the woman, taunting her, willing her to do something. The

woman's face showed all the right signs of alarm, her fists

clenching and unclenching at her sides. Viv knew she had to

choose her next words carefully. Almost in a whisper, she said, 'So

was rape part of the game plan?' Viv never took her eyes off the

woman, and watched as fear flitted across her face. 'You going to

stand by and watch while he rapes another woman?' With each

question she lowered her voice for the word 'rape'.

The woman slowly stepped away from the door.

He yelled at her, 'Don't you dare!'

The woman's face flashed with anger. And she took another

step. 'Let her go.' Her voice unequivocal.

Viv gently gathered her breath. His grip gave slightly. He was obviously astonished to be addressed in this way. Viv remained still as he screwed up his eyes, and removed his hand from his flies.

He tightened his grip on Viv's arm. 'She needs to be taught a lesson.'

The woman snorted. 'I don't think so. She's right, this . . .' she nodded at his groin, 'wasn't in my game plan. Let her go.' Her voice remained steady.

This was more than Viv could have hoped for. And she was able to think while the secretary did her work for her. Sanchez suddenly punched Viv's shoulder again, and she almost fainted with the pain. She felt her colour drain and again bile rose. Huge though he was, between them they might be able to overcome him, although if she managed to get herself loose, her injured shoulder would prevent her doing much.

As if she had read Viv's mind, the woman stepped forward again and with a smooth sweep grabbed a Big Bertha from the bag of clubs and took aim at Sanchez' shins. She was no golfer but who was watching?

He screamed. 'Nooooo!'

But she was well past the point of no return, and as she made contact with his thigh-bone he went down squealing like a pig, releasing Viv in the process. Viv staggered to avoid him and almost fell, but the woman, breathing as if she'd fought a prize fight, caught Viv's elbow so she remained upright. Viv hobbled round to the telephone and dialled 999. The woman headed to the door, still holding the club, so Viv wasn't inclined to pursue he

Viv shouted into the phone, 'Police emergency at the Knightsfiel

golf pro shop!'

At first the woman struggled to undo the catch on the door bt

as soon as she managed, she glanced back at Sanchez, who ashe

and breathless still squirmed on the floor. 'The way you sai

'secretary' − such contempt. I hadn't heard that tone since I was a

school.' She nodded towards Viv. 'She's right. I was only a puppe

to you.'

He gasped but nothing more came out and he fainted.

Rage rose up from the base of Viv's spine and she steppe

round to where he lay and sank a brutal kick into his groin. Wher

he was going he wouldn't be needing those.

Chapter Twenty-Five

There was something honourable about the fact that the woman had left the Big Bertha propped neatly by the side of the door. Not exactly the work of a hardened criminal. Viv plonked herself down on a tweed-covered chair, designed for people buying wildly expensive golf shoes, and put her head in her hands. There wasn't a muscle in her body not smarting. She wondered what their relationship had been; if it had been a tempestuous affair, or if that was what he'd been hoping for. The woman had had competition, what with Geraldine and the wife. A siren wailing in the distance was such a welcome sound that she felt her eyes daring to fill. When the door opened an officer ran in, and immediately knelt by Sanchez.

Viv could see how the situation looked and how easily it would be interpreted as her fault.

'What's been going on here?'

A second officer stood on the threshold with the door half open and spoke over his shoulder to the grounds-man outside. They seemed familiar with each other and Viv saw the officer squeeze the grounds-man's hand. More than chums. Viv smiled.

The first officer spoke into his headset. 'We need an ambulance here at Knightsfield. Asap. One male unconscious.'

Viv 's anger began to bubble. 'He's probably faking it.'

The officer shot her a look, which said, 'I'll get to you in a minute, lady.'

'Look at me. D'you think I did all of this to myself?'

As he was about to answer a bulky shadow appeared in the doorway. DS Sandra Nicholson strode in, wearing civvies.

The officer said, 'And who might you be?'

Red, as she was known to Viv, flashed her ID, and the guy nodded. 'You're looking a bit the worse for wear, Doc. Maybe you shouldn't be allowed out.'

Viv's eyes filled again. Never had she seen such a welcome sight. Choking on her relief she said, 'How did you . . .'

Red grinned. 'Marconi's still playing the wild man. He called, said you might be needing help.'

'But how could you know where . . .'

Red nodded to the grounds-man outside. 'He phoned in to the local station and gave the registration of a car that Marconi had tagged. The rest as they say is . . . just the beginning. But let's get you sorted. That shoulder's not looking too cocky.'

When Viv went to stand up her legs gave way and she staggered back onto the chair.

'Whoa there, Doc. You stay put. I'll get you an ambulance.'

'I'm not going anywhere with that.' Viv pointed at Sanchez, who was coming round.

'Feeling's mutual, you filthy bitch.'

Red stared from one to the other.

Viv watched as comprehension flitted over Red's face.

Sanchez' zip was still undone and Viv's shirt and trousers were dishevelled.

Red raised her eyebrows in a question and Viv nodded. 'There was another . . .'

'Yes, we got her as she was racing up the drive. She was in the tagged car.'

'She tried to . . .'

Red's tone softened and she positioned herself between Viv and Sanchez. 'Don't worry. We'll get to the whys and what fors. You just chill.'

A young female PC was instructed to sit with Viv while Red took over the admin. Another siren marked the arrival of the ambulance. Sanchez wasn't moving anywhere with his mashed thigh, but it didn't stop him from making promises of retribution through gritted teeth. The sooner they got him removed the better for his own sake, since he was digging his own injudicious grave where he was.

Wrapped in a blanket Viv was accompanied by a female paramedic to the ambulance.

Red nodded to her and said, 'You going to be okay?'

Viv stared back and bit her cheek. Red threw her car keys to a PC and said, 'Follow the ambulance.' Then she crouched in beside Viv on a bench that wasn't intended for people her size. Red was all muscle and stood almost six feet tall, a mane of dark ginger curls was held neatly at the base of her occipital bone by a bronze clip. A fine-boned freckled face seemed incongruently pretty for her size. Viv imagined a more horsey face for that body.

'Thanks, Red. How many times is it now?'

Red winked. 'Getting to be too many to count, Doc. People d(

all manner of things to get my attention, but I've got to give it t(

you girl for creativity.'

She rubbed Viv's hand and Viv put her other hand over the top

'Thank God that woman, the secretary, decided to switch teams . .

although it'd take a certain kind of psycho to stand and watcl

another woman being raped.'

'Don't you believe it. I've seen more than my fair share o:

women who'd do worse things than any man.' Red shook her head

'D'you think he'd have gone through with it?'

Viv thought for a minute. 'He'd got himself into a frenzy. A

state where his rage had become sexual.' Viv pulled her little picl

out of the heel of her boot and held it up. 'This was all I had left.'

Red took it and touched the point of it with her index finger

She immediately drew blood. 'What had you planned to do witl

it?'

'The only place I know where it would make a dramati(

difference would be his eye.'

Red squirmed and handed it back. She sucked her finger an(

nodded. 'Yep, I can see that working.'

'Thank God Big Bertha came to the rescue. It would have taker

every cell of hatred in my body to stick that in someone's eye.' She

grinned. 'I was close, though. The odd thing is that when you're ii

the middle of an attack, you're not quite convinced that it is reall] happening. It was as if I was having an out-of-body experience. Sure, he's hauling at my zip and then at his own, but it seemed unreal. Almost farcical.'

Red nodded again, 'You'll not be the first woman who has shut off her reason when being attacked.'

'No, no, it wasn't like that.'

Red interrupted. 'Yeah, and you're not the first to say that either. Let's wait until we've had you sorted before we get down to details.'

From that area of East Lothian, the Royal Infirmary was easily accessible, a quick journey. Viv was taken straight to A&E. There were no smokers outside the building, and the waiting area was quiet. She saw no sign of Sanchez and was grateful for it.

The first doctor to look at her shoulder was a slightly built Asian man. 'It's dislocated. I can reset it without anaesthetic but it will hurt.'

Viv looked at Red, but Red turned away, obviously squeamish at the thought. 'Go ahead. It can't be much more painful than it is now.'

'Oh, you'll be instantly relieved,' the doctor reassured her.

'Okay, go for it.' She clenched her jaw and squeezed her eyes tight shut.

Red took Viv's other hand as the doctor pulled and turned Viv's arm in ways that seemed impossible for any human body. Then he did a manoeuvre so quickly that neither Viv nor Red could believe it was over. The relief was instantaneous.

Viv looked at her shoulder, back in its normal position. 'Wow Is that it?'

The doctor made a tiny bow with his head and gave her a sligh smile. She could see he was chuffed with what he'd done. 'Wel done. I didn't feel anything.'

'You might later.' He nodded and left.

A nurse bustled in and began to clean up her cuts and bruises This was excruciating and she winced with each gentle stroke.

Red laughed. 'Man up, Doc. I thought we'd be peeling you of the roof with what he's just done. I couldn't even look.'

Red's phone rang and the nurse shot her a side glare. Red held i up and said, 'I'll have to take this.' And headed into the corridor When she returned she was blowing out a long breath and shaking her head. 'You gotta give it to some of these guys.'

Viv's brows furrowed in a question.

Red gestured to the right. 'Our man is still yelling that he's going to sort you out.' She tutted. 'Cuffs not making a single bit o difference. I think he's suffering from God syndrome. What dic you do to him?' Then she raised her hands and batted Viv's potential answer into submission. 'Later. Later. I'm guessing he'l end up in a psych ward.'

'That'd be ironic, famous neuro-psychologist on the wrong side of the door of a locked ward. Don't suppose he'll be the first. Fine line between sane and insane.'

Once the nurse was finished Viv thanked her, and she and Rec made their way to the front entrance. How extraordinary it was tha

242

hospitals dealt with the beginning and end of life and everything in between. Within a few seconds Red's car pulled up with the PC at the wheel. He leapt out to open the door.

Red waved him off and opened the back door for Viv. 'Chill, you can drive us back to St Leonard's. I'd like to find out more about our lunatic professor. He can't possibly be what he says he is.' She grinned at Viv. 'Unless you want to go straight home?'

'No chance.'

Red rubbed her hands together. 'I thought as much.'

Viv was shattered but desperate to find out what, if anything, Sanchez had been up to. 'Sure, I'm up for that. A few Paracetamol will do the trick.'

'Absolutely sure?'

Viv nodded. 'Yep. I'll let you know if I'm done in.' She tried to stretch her arm and wondered how long it would be before she'd be able to cut layers again. She imagined herself in the shower, but felt queasy at the idea of water gushing through the gash on her head. She tried to recall the worst of the attack, starting in the car. She must have pushed her elbow up to protect her head from the crow bar, or whatever metal pole he'd been wielding. If she hadn't reacted so quickly, he could easily have killed her. But that didn't make sense, he'd needed her alive.

'You okay, Doc?' Red looked concerned.

'Sure, just feeling manky, but no worries, an extra hour won't kill me.'

Chapter Twenty-Six

As they pulled into the car park at St Leonards, Mac stood leaning on the roof of his Audi with a mobile clamped to his ear. When he noticed Viv he cut the call and marched round to open the car door for her.

She put her good hand up to stop him from speaking. In the pas when Mac had turned up to rescue her she'd started to bubble and here was certainly not the place for that caper.

'I'm fine. On a scale of one to ten I'm probably at five, six at a push. So whatever you do don't be nice to me.'

Red flashed him a look, which Viv caught and understood to be a back-off-for-now gesture. The four then entered St Leonards with Viv, Red and Mac making their way through the busy reception Once beyond a set of secure doors they took the stairs up to an office with a conference table, chairs, a coffee machine and a bank of windows facing onto the main road.

Viv collapsed into a chair. 'Right, let's get this done.'

'D'you need coffee or something to eat?'

Viv glanced at the machine. It was still early enough in the day for the brew to be drinkable. 'Why not?'

Just then the PC knocked on the door and brought in a plate o: pastries. Viv spotted one with custard in it and pointed. 'I think that one's got my name on it.'

Red shook her head. 'What are you like? I'd be feeling like rolling into my own grave if I'd been through what you have.'

Viv threw her a weak smile. 'Stamina's not what it might be, but still I couldn't overlook a custard pastry.'

Mac said, 'Look, we need to rule Sanchez out of all the stuff that happened up in Doune. It's bad enough with the beating, kidnapping and attempted rape; but we've got all the attacks on you and the property, not to mention the dog.'

At the mention of Moll, Viv welled up. Instinctively her hands reached for her face. She winced and with her good hand she rubbed the bits that she could.

Mac continued. 'You sure you're okay to do this? It could easily wait.'

Red glanced at Mac and shook her head. 'The sooner we get this over the better.'

So with a recorder on and Red with a pen poised, Viv began to tell all that she could remember; from the first attack on the drive at Sal's, through the stone toppling on Inchmaholme, the slashed tyre, the next attack at Sal's, being driven off the road on her way home from doing Gail's hair, and finally the kidnap. 'By the way, what have you got on the guy that was found in his office? Who was he?'

Mac said, 'Whoever he is, he's related to Sanchez.'

Viv nodded and continued. 'Makes sense . . . But listen, I don't think the incidents up at Inchmaholme had anything to do with him. I think whoever did those intended a malicious attack on the police. It wouldn't surprise me if Mr Byron Ponsonby wa responsible for those. Sanchez' attacks were personal. He's totall; homophobic. I mean we are talkin' pathologically homophobic And I think we'll find that he was, or still is, married to my e: Dawn's sister. ' She saw Red glance at Mac, who said, 'You knov about Dawn, right?'

Red replied slowly, 'Well, I knew that there had been someone. Unable to find the right word she hesitated. 'Significant.'

Viv smiled. 'You could say that. But she's proving to be mor(significant in death than when we were together. Sanchez got i into his head that the family, i.e. him, should have inheritec Dawn's legacy. Nerve. He's not even related. His wife is but no him, and as far as I know he's no longer with the wife.' She shool her head and instantly regretted it.

Both Red and Mac raised their eyebrows in a question. Rec said, 'And?'

'And nothing. Dawn left everything she owned to me. If I'(known just how much hassle it would be I'd have refused . . . com(to think about it I did refuse, but the solicitor was having none of i and set up the trust. Told me to forget about it.' Her eyes ros(towards the ceiling. 'I wonder.'

Mac said, 'What do you wonder?'

'I wonder if the solicitor has anything to do with this. Given tha· it was so easy for Sanchez to get into his system. Aren't they supposed to have all kinds of protection? Actually forget that. I'n just thinking out loud. Sal's solicitor's account was also hacked

Funnily enough Sanchez doesn't strike me as a guy with enough endurance to be a hacker.' Then she smiled. 'It's probably the secretary.' She nodded. 'Yep. He'll have exploited her skills and fed her a line about . . .'

'Go on,' Red said.

'Well, by the time we were all cosying up in the pro's shop, the secretary was wavering. Her resolve was visibly crumbling. Every time he opened his mouth her eyes showed her disbelief. So whatever fairy tale he'd fed her wasn't coming true. What he was doing to me didn't fit with her expectations. I'm grateful that she walloped him with that club, though, because I was definitely flagging.'

Mac said, 'A bit like now, I guess.'

'No, nothing like now. Then, I was up against a psycho who was desperate to kill me, but he knew if he did he wouldn't get anything. There's nothing more frustrating than an opponent who has a psychological advantage like that. I could see it in his eyes. He'd lost the plot . . . I wonder why they took me away down there? D'you think it was because the course had been cleared for the tournament?' She didn't wait for an answer. 'The course would never be that empty ever. But . . . is he a member?'

Mac said, 'I'll find out.' He stood and went to the door and spoke for a moment to a PC in the corridor, then turned back, continuing, 'I don't get it. Don't surgeons get paid mega bucks? And what about the old Hippocratic oath and all that?' He shook his head. 'I think you're right, Viv. He must be a psycho. I get that

he's greedy and fancies a bit of extra cash, but the homophobi
hate crime is in that kind of category. Imagine working as hard a
he's had to to become a surgeon and blowing it for the sake of
few quid.' He looked at Viv.

She was looking sheepish. 'It's more than just a few quid
There's land . . . and . . .' She faltered, embarrassed. 'Well, th
details don't matter. He'll never get his hands on it. The whol
purpose of Dawn leaving it to me was so that her family wouldn't
She had no other reason.'

Mac and Red laughed in unison. Mac said, 'You think?'

Viv was definitely close to the end of her tether. 'Trust me; he
motives weren't gracious.'

Red said, 'I think we've got enough to be going on with. Th
last thing we need is a DNA swab.'

'What? Why do you . . . for Christ sake, my details are alread
in the system.'

Mac confirmed this with a nod to Red.

.'Okay, Doc. I'll take you home.'

Mac said, 'You're all right. I'll take her.'

Red looked put out.

Viv glanced from one to the other. 'For fuck sake! Does i
matter who takes me? As long as someone does, and soon.'

Viv emerged after a few days cocooned in her duvet. She plugge
her landline in and put her mobile on to charge, a significant sig
of healing. Shaking her head proved it was still tender. Sh

stretched her arm as high as she could – better. The minute power was coursing through the phone it began beeping. Texts and messages just kept on arriving. She wasn't ready to hear them yet and set about making espresso and hot buttered toast. As she waited for the coffee to drip through, she thought of the boatman, Byron Ponsonby. It struck her that there must be a limit to the reasons for breaking into a grave. These days taking a body for medical science was off the menu, but searching for grave goods was not. It might have been that Edward BP knew that one or both of the bodies had been buried with special items. And grave goods from the twentieth century wouldn't mean loaves of bread or libations for gods in the afterlife; more likely to be precious and non-perishable. Jewellery, money, even documents were likely contenders. Pets, at a stretch, but who would want to dig those up?

Armed with breakfast she padded through to the sitting room, booted up her laptop, and settled on the couch. Her laptop pinged continuously. Emails, like texts and messages, could wait until the coffee had worked its magic. Meanwhile she Googled Byron Ponsonby again. She couldn't find the article about the land dispute that she'd seen last time. She scrolled and scrolled until something else caught her eye, an article on Lady Byron Ponsonby, still alive and kicking and living on Sheriffmuir. Viv had noticed some mature specimen trees on the hill behind Maggie's bothy; non-native species were usually a sign of a big house.

She clicked onto Google maps. This was her kind of research. What was not to like about armchair archaeology? Sure enough, a turreted Victorian pile was hidden in the trees. Not huge; probabl₁ built as a shooting lodge. She homed in and saw that th₁ photograph had been taken in summertime. The fields were yellov and not bright green as they'd been last week. She clicked back t₁ the article and read on. It turned out that the estate was called Ochi Brae and was owned by a family called Bruce. Lady Byro₁ Ponsonby had first been Lady Bruce. It looked as if she'd inherite₁ the estate, and yes, it was a shooting estate with a grouse moo₁ over the back of the hill. It also included a number of cottages, th₁ Inn, and Maggie's bothy. Viv said to the screen, 'I wonder if you₁ inheritance cost you as much as mine has?'

She convinced herself that this was all relevant because i connected Byron Ponsonby of the lakeside dwelling to th₁ archaeological dig on Sheriffmuir. From this site Viv typed i₁ 'Bruce of Sheriffmuir' and a whole ream of articles came up including information that the Byron Ponsonbys still had a₁ 'interest' in the estate. She raised her eyebrows and grinned. Thi₁ could take some time so she refilled her coffee cup, pushed th₁ central heating button to override and wrapped her duvet round he₁ until it kicked back in.

Chapter Twenty-Seven

Historical land auctions where locals had to bid for the grazing, an old article from the *Stirling Observer* about some minor Royal or other coming to shoot, and a couple of mentions of the Byron Ponsonbys were some of the pieces she ploughed through. She even read a story about Lady BP opening the Doune and Dunblane Show, an agricultural event that had attracted the world and his wife if the crowded sepia photographs were anything to go by. Viv was hooked. Old photographs always fascinated her and now that she could put faces to Sir Malcolm Byron Ponsonby and his stunning wife Lady Claire Bruce, it made the puzzle all the more worthy of unpicking.

Byron Ponsonby had made money in the tobacco trade in the west of Scotland. His knighthood went to his grave with him. Lady Claire, on the other hand, was ancient, Scottish landed gentry, her title was inherited. So that's why there's still a Lady Byron. Ponsonby living up at Sheriffmuir now, thought Viv. She found the Inn's website and jotted down the postcode. If it was part of an estate, all the buildings would have the same code. Definitely worth searching for the current Lady BP.

'Oh, my God! Well, who'd have thought.' Viv stretched for her mobile and pressed Mac's fast dial.

'Viv. Thank God. I've left you so many messages.'

She interrupted him. 'Yeah, yeah. You should know better tha to bug a woman who needs her beauty sleep.'

'Beauty sleep, you're like Rip van bloody Winkle.'

She smiled at his concern. 'I'm fine now. Aching but fine. Bu listen, I've been doing a bit of Googling and guess what?' Sh heard him sighing. 'Who's rattled your cage this morning? I wa just going to say that I've found . . .'

He interrupted her. 'Look, Viv, I'm busy right now, but w could grab a coffee later. I'll be through here at five; how about nip up then?'

She hesitated. 'Okay. Do that. Why don't you bring a pizza an I'll see if I can find a bottle of . . . '

Again he cut her off. It was so unlike him. 'I've got somethin on tonight.'

Something in his tone made her stomach tighten. 'What, like date kind of something?'

'Yeah, well, kind of.'

'Surely you know whether it's a date or not. I pity the woman i you've not yet decided.'

He came back at her. 'It's not as simple as that.'

Viv wasn't enjoying this one little bit. 'Okay, coffee it is. Bu actually I could just tell you now.'

'No can do. See you at five.' He cut the call.

Viv stared at her mobile in disbelief. Mac didn't hang up. Ma didn't date. Or he hadn't since they'd been back working together In two or more years he hadn't mentioned a single love interest well not in the present tense. She placed her hand on her belly as if it would calm her mind. 'Mac with a date? Mac in a relationship? No way. Yes way. Shit.' This news certainly shaved the edge off her excitement about the BPs. She repeated to herself, 'Mac with a date. A real live date.' She fleetingly wondered who it could be, and imagined what they might do. Disturbing. A vision of Mac laying his elegant hand on the small of another woman's back made her shudder. What the fuck was going on? She'd had her chance. Jealousy wasn't an option with mates.

She loafed around, trying to muster enthusiasm for her earlier discovery, but her heart wasn't in it, so she set about answering emails and checking text messages. These distracted her for a little while but a vision of Mac with his hand on the small of a fantasy woman's back kept creeping into her mind. She rubbed her eyes. What the hell was wrong with her? She didn't want Mac, but she obviously wasn't too pleased if someone else did. She gave herself a talking to and eventually crawled back into bed, exhausted.

She woke to an insistent blast on her buzzer. The clock read 16.30. She staggered to the intercom and spoke to the person downstairs. 'Whoever you are I don't have the author . . .'

Mac said, 'Open the door. It's me.'

She looked down at herself and her eyes almost popped out. 'Come up. Take your time. I was just about to get in the shower.' She lied. Leaving the door on the snib she dived into the bathroom. When she had finished her ablutions and scrubbed her teeth, she found Mac in the kitchen browsing through an ancient copy of a trashy magazine, with a pot of coffee beginning to gurgle on the stove.

She rubbed gingerly at the hair around her wound.

'That still looks pretty painful.'

'It's much better. If you'd seen it yesterday with all the blood still crusted round it, it looked much worse, like a wound from a movie set only not . . .' She heard herself babbling. She couldn' make eye contact with him, but had to slide by him to get to the cupboard with the cups. The smell of him made her swallow. He shifted his chair to let her reach in. She felt her colour rising hating the proximity.

'You all right there?' he asked.

And too defensively she replied, 'Why wouldn't I be?'

'Eh, well, because only a few days ago you were beaten to a pulp.'

Of course his question was entirely innocent. 'I'm healing well. As you see.'

She lifted her damp hair back off her face, exposing the gash.

'Ouch! Still looks bad. You're braver than I would be.'

Now she knew he was kidding. Mac had seen some serious action in his time and Viv had seen his scars.

'So what did you find out that you were so keen to tell me?'

Again too defensively she said, 'I thought you'd want to know. The Byron Ponsonbys own all the land up at Sheriffmuir. And Lady BP, whoever the hell she is, still lives there. I'm guessing in the shooting lodge up in the woods beyond Maggie's bothy.'

He nodded. 'You're right. Lady BP does still live up there, but not in the lodge. Maggie O' the Bog . . . is Lady Byron Ponsonby.'

It took a few seconds for this to sink in. 'Maggie is Lady Byron Ponsonby?'

He nodded and smiled, delighted at being able to surprise her. 'I got a couple of PCs to do a bit of digging and they found an old piece from . . .'

She interrupted him. 'The *Stirling Observer*? Probably the same one that I found. But how did they discover that Maggie was a Byron Ponsonby?'

'Easy. I got a phone number for her and rang and asked if I was speaking to Lady Byron Ponsonby. At first she said who's asking, but when I said the police she relented.'

'Okay. So she and Edward are . . .? Husband and wife, brother and sister, cousins? What?'

'Brother and sister. Neither married.'

'What was all that stuff about all those generations living in that bothy?'

'Well, she didn't actually say that. She just said that they'd been there, worked the land . . .'

'She was deliberately trying to mislead us.' She blew out a breath. 'So has she got something to do with Edward? I mean, are they in cahoots?'

'In some way, but we haven't worked it out yet. You see if all they've done is look inside a family grave, they by rights haven't done anything illegal.' He grinned. 'But if they stole something

from the grave. For example, a skull, but more importantly on
with gold teeth in it . . .'

She gasped and screwed up her face. 'No way. Why the hel
would they do that?'

'Perhaps they thought they'd find other grave goods and didn't
then decided that they might as well have what treasure there was
We're searching his cabin as we speak.'

'What, for gold teeth?' she laughed.

'Yep! Apparently toffs used to spend quite a bit of money
having teeth removed and gold ones put in their place. Very few
people are blessed with the kind of gnashers you have.' He looked
at her, but she avoided his eye.

Her colour rose again. She wished he hadn't paid her a
compliment, however backhanded it was, but it was what she liked
about him. There was no side to him. Her teeth were one of he
best assets, but still, he shouldn't have said. Should is shit, Viv, she
reminded herself. If he wasn't going on a date, would she have
noticed? Would she have blushed like a stupid schoolgirl? No and
no. Get a grip, girl.

She busied herself organising the coffee. 'Let's take it through.'
She nodded to the hallway and carrying both their cups wandered
ahead.

'You got any of that crystal sugar left?'

'No,' she replied. She thought he sighed and threw over her
shoulder, 'First world problem, Mac, not the end of the world as
we know it. If you check the top cupboard to the right of the

window you'll find some molasses sugar. Try that.'

When he joined her he took up more space than she liked. He seemed totally disproportionate to the room. As if the room had shrunk. She perched on the windowsill, the space furthest away from where he plonked himself onto the couch.

'You've done well to find out . . .'

'Piss off, you patronising sod. You've already got everything that I found.'

'I know, but it doesn't do any harm having you back it up.'

'I still can't believe they opened up a grave for a few teeth. There's bound to be more to it. I mean, who'd risk jail for a few bits of gold?'

'Oh the weight of the gold will be worth a few bob.' He blew over the top of his cup.

She'd seen him do this a hundred times, but now it looked so delicate. She felt herself being charmed by it. By the way he wrapped his long fingers round the cup. By the way he hitched up his trousers to prevent them from becoming kneed. By the way he pushed his hair out of his eyes. She internally bawled at herself to grow up.

He smiled as if he noticed she was tussling with something. 'You okay?'

'Why d'you keeping asking me that? Of course I'm okay.'

He shrugged and raised a placatory hand. 'Okay. Well if you're that okay maybe you could do a bit more digging. Online of course.'

She caught something in his tone that meant the words had more meaning to them. 'D'you mean my kind of digging?'

He sighed and shook his head. 'I don't want to influence what you look at online, but if there did happen to be something beyond teeth . . .'

'Ah! Okay. I gotcha.'

He swiped his hand across his forehead in mock relief. 'Good.' He stood. 'I'd better be going then.' He didn't move towards the door, but kept staring at her as if imploring her to say something.

She looked at her feet. 'Right. I'll see what I can do.' Then she pushed herself off the windowsill.

He strolled down the hall. She followed. He opened the door and stepped onto the landing, at which point she sighed, feeling on the right side of safety, in no danger of reaching out to him. He raised his hand in the slightest wave, but didn't look back.

She closed the door and with her back against it slid to the floor and put her head in her hands. 'What an arse? How could I be such an arse?' Then as if he might have heard her she turned and stared at the door. 'Right, get yourself together.' And with this she returned to her laptop in the sitting room. At a loss for inspiration she typed 'grave goods in the nineteenth century?' into Google and was amazed at the types of things that showed up. First up, it was illegal to bury anything with a body, since it was believed to be contaminating, but lots of people ignored this and requested that they be buried with objects that had meaning for them. Even Queen Victoria insisted on having goods in her coffin with her.

The Byron Ponsonbys needn't have been any different. Perhaps there was a family story about what they took to the grave, or their wills would reveal what was left. Someone must know. The internet was addictive and she scrolled and scrolled, occasionally hooked by a story that although interesting, turned out to be a dead end. Eventually, with a bit of searching on the wrong side of legality, Viv managed to find first their death certificates, then by sheer fluke a letter of wishes belonging to, or ascribed to, Lady Byron Ponsonby. Mac wouldn't want to know how she got the information and she'd be accused of moral bankruptcy but he'd still want whatever she found. She marvelled at how easy it was to get such personal information. Even Sanchez had managed to find her and Sal's accounts. Her justification for this kind of snooping was, she believed, for the greater good, unlike Sanchez who'd done it entirely for his own gain. She could justify almost anything, if she had to.

Lady BP had hoped to be buried with a few pieces, one ring that had belonged to her grandmother – no description given, the family would be expected to know which ring she meant – a carved ivory box – no mention of size or contents. She also wanted to be buried in her cream silk dupion dress and a lace jabot. Viv wondered if she'd got her wishes, and if she had what kind of state that frock would be in after decades in the ground. She glanced at the time on her laptop and was surprised to see how late it was. She'd managed to kill almost four hours on this search and felt peckish. She hadn't eaten since the buttered toast late morning, and the coffee she'd had with Mac had long since ceased to give he veins a boost.

The fridge didn't offer anything much, but there was som deliciously smelly cheese that would do with oatcakes. She gulpe down a glass of fizzy water, then refilled the glass and took i through to the sitting room with the cheese and biscuits. Sh flicked on the TV and scanned for something that would take he mind off the Byron Ponsonbys. She heard the ping of an emai arriving in her inbox, but continued to search for something decen on the TV. There was nothing, so she went to find out who ha sent the email. It was from Mac. He'd forwarded a report by th archaeologists from Sheriffmuir. She looked at the time. What wa he doing working? The report noted that the bone they'd identifie as newer than the rest was a section of fractured jaw. She gaspe when she read the next line. It appeared to have recent scratche from a tool, possibly a Phillips screwdriver. Viv shook her head i disbelief. 'You couldn't make it up,' she said to the screen, an continued to read the report. Their interpretation was that a eighteen-carat gold tooth had been gouged out. Traces of gol were still evident in the cavity. 'Oh, my God. How desperate wer they?' She checked the time again. Ten-thirty. What the heck wa Mac doing sending her an email in the middle of his date? He fingers hovered above the keyboard before she wrote him a repl and clicked send. If he was with someone he should have hi phone off.

Viv sat with a note pad and jotted down a few hypotheses, th kinds of 'what if?' and 'what else could that mean?' questions. If Maggie and Edward were brother and sister she might find something about them online. It didn't take long. He'd been out of the family frame for thirty plus years. 'The Black Sheep.' At sea? She rubbed her temples, wary of getting too close to the scab, which became itchy when she went anywhere near it, a sign it was healing well. She thought she'd call it a night, but before she did she attached her findings to an email and sent it to Mac. It had barely bounced off the satellite, twenty-three thousand miles away, when an answer pinged into her box. She mused at the miracle of technology and read the message.

'Nightcap?'

'What the . . .' She continued to stare at the message while mulling over her options. He wouldn't know whether she'd read it or not. 'Your call, Vivian,' she whispered to the screen. Her stomach was fluttering, but she quickly ascribed that to the idea of conquest and not the reality of Mac. No chase, meant, no point. Was her attitude outdated; shouldn't she try to get over it? She reflected on the absence of success in her relationship department. This could be her chance for change; or would it add to her list of failures? She closed the lid of the laptop and headed through to the bedroom. She climbed beneath the duvet and was stretching to switch the lamp off, but hesitated, 'What a fuckwit you are. He's only asking for a nightcap not, "what are you doing 'til death do us part?"' She threw the duvet off and went back through to the laptop. She typed, 'Just about to hit the sack.' And clicked send.

She waited. Nothing. She waited a bit longer. Then just as she wa᪄ about to close everything down her inbox pinged.

'Too late. Just parking up at Learmonth. See you soon. M.'

She frowned. He obviously hadn't read her reply. Miffed tha᪄ the choice was no longer hers she retreated to the comfort of he᪄ duvet. She lay in the dark, her magpie brain busy with images o᪄ recent events. Beams from the occasional set of headlights flitte᪄ across the walls, lighting up objects on the chest of drawers. A᪄ small Clarice Cliff vase caught her eye. She sighed, reassured to be᪄ in familiar surroundings, safe. She thought about the women tha᪄ she'd shared the container with. What had been their fate? She wa᪄ in no doubt that whatever it was it would be worse than her own᪄ At least for the time being they weren't for sale, they weren't the᪄ property of some pimp whose only care was for a buck. Sanche᪄ was just like a pimp. Would a judge be lenient because he was a᪄ doctor? Would he find a good enough lawyer to get him off on a᪄ technicality? Mac had shored up enough evidence to make tha᪄ difficult, but the law was not about justice. She rubbed her eyes t᪄ try to eliminate a vision of Sanchez' leering face. Her thought᪄ returned to Mac. She was being stupid. What she had with Ma᪄ was mutuality, which was surely more desirable than any fling.

She rolled onto her good side and pulled her knees up to he᪄ chest. Why did she feel judged for being on her own? Wasn'᪄ being single the new black and not the pathological state tha᪄ Bridget Jones made it out to be? Although at times, not times like᪄ now, but at other times, having someone around was a comfort.

Gabriella came to mind. How was she doing? Beneath the question was the fact that she hadn't seen Gabriella around. Was the shop thriving? If not, would Gabriella be forced to move on? With this notion a strange kind of territorial relief seeped into her. Her head swam with the ghosts of girlfriends and boyfriends past as if they had been assigned to the same chamber of nightmares as Sanchez and her experience in the container. She hauled the duvet over her head, time to count sheep off the lorry and back onto the hill.

ABOUT THE AUTHOR

Vicki Clifford was born in Edinburgh and until recently taught Religious Studies at the University of Stirling. She has an unusual background as a freelance hairdresser with a Ph.D on psychoanalysis from the University of Edinburgh. She published her first book, *Freud's Converts* in 2007. She lives in Perthshire, Scotland. *Digging Up The Dead* is the third of the Viv Fraser Mysteries.

ACKNOWLEDGMENTS

I would like to thank Nicola Wood. Sue Harvey, Belinda Stansfield, Carolyn Smith, Pauline Wright and David Reith for their continued support. Without Robin Chapman Campbell with me every step of the way life would be too dull for words.

CONTACT

https://www.facebook.com/Vicki-Clifford-Author-372804446203766/?ref=hl

Twitter @VicClifford

Digging Up The Dead

Made in the USA
Charleston, SC
09 December 2015